Christina thinks she's indestructible—but she's wrong

Stepping onto the roof, Christina ducked her head away from the pelting rain.

The kitten mewed plaintively, clinging to the drain as if it were the only thing keeping him from being washed away.

"Everything's okay, Raindrop," Christina crooned. She reached with one hand and scooped up the whimpering ball of wet fur. Cradling him in one arm, she began her return trip in tiny, careful steps.

At the window, Katie reached out. Christina handed her the kitten.

With her back still pressed against the outside wall, Christina heaved a sigh of relief. She'd made it. She reached up to steady herself as she turned. She took a cautious step—and the tile beneath her shot out from under her foot.

"No!" Katie screamed as Christina fell.

Christina cried out in shock and terror as she hit the tile roof on her back. Then she realized she was sliding, sliding fast.

She clawed at the tiles, desperate for something to hold on to. But there was nothing.

The Forgotten Angel

FOREVER ANGELS

The Forgotten Angel

Suzanne Weyn

Troll

Contents of this edition copyright © Troll Communications L.L.C. Watermill Press is an imprint and registered trademark of Troll Communications L.L.C.

Text copyright © 1996 by Chardiet Unlimited, Inc., and Suzanne Weyn.
Cover illustration copyright © 1996 by Mark English.
Cover border photography by Katrina.
Angel stickers (GS16) copyright © 1991 by Gallery Graphics, Inc., Noel, MO 64854. Used with permission.

Published by Troll Communications L.L.C.

Printed in the United States of America.

10 9 8 7 6 5 4 3 2

The Forgotten Angel

1

Christina stretched her arms out in front of her, waving them, searching the darkness. "Mom!" she called, her voice rising to a frightened pitch. "Mom, are you there? Mom, answer me! Please!"

Her eyes strained hard, desperate to pick any form at all out of the jet black darkness that encased her. But she could see nothing. In her fear and eagerness to find her mother, she moved forward, shuffling her feet to keep in touch with the ground, the only solid thing she could be sure of.

Where was she? She'd never seen darkness like this. How had she gotten here? She had no idea.

Normally, even with the lights out, Christina could always discern the forms of things once her eyes adjusted to the dark. There'd be a glint of pale light outlining the edge of a table or the side of a dresser. At the very least, there might be a bit of moonbeam filtering through a curtain. Light from another room would slip, in a determined sliver, under the door.

This was different.

It was absolute blackness with no shading or form anywhere. A complete absence of light. And it was terrifying.

"Mom," she called again, her voice shaky. She didn't like the quivering, childish sound of her own voice. She couldn't give in to fear now. She had to be brave and get out of this darkness somehow.

Christina wasn't sure why she felt the urgent need to find her mother. There was no reason for her to think her mother was even nearby. Yet she knew she must find her. But where could she be? How would she ever locate her in this complete darkness? "Mom! Mom!" Her words came out as a plaintive shout.

Arms still outstretched, she took several cautious steps forward. As she moved through the blackness, she remembered how once, when she was four, she'd gotten lost at the mall. It surprised her that her voice now—at thirteen—sounded so much like her younger voice had sounded back then—full of tight fear. And so very childlike.

Where could she be? Why was there nothing to hold on to? Why wasn't she bumping into anything? Was this an empty room? Frustration filled her. Where was she?

Then she saw it and took a long, hopeful breath.

A vibrant door-sized rectangle of light shone several yards ahead of her. It shimmered, yet had sharp edges, as if it came from inside the open doorway of a room ablaze with candles.

With arms still outstretched, Christina stumbled toward it, her heart banging with excitement.

At last! Here was relief from the thick, impenetrable, oppressing darkness!

What was in the room? What would she find?

Christina stepped into the doorway and spread her arms wide. "I knew it!" she cried in a voice rich with deep joy. "Somehow I always knew it!"

2

Christina shot forward to a sitting position in her bed. It was still dark, but now she could see the familiar shapes of her tall pinewood dresser, the long mirror on the back of her bedroom door, her window with a moonlight-filled lower pane, and a rustic wooden rocker beside it. She gripped her light Navajo-print blanket in both hands just to feel it, to be sure she was really awake.

"An angel," she murmured, recalling the joyful vision she'd seen in the light-filled room. She'd dreamed of a welcoming, gorgeous angel. She saw that radiant angel again in her mind's eye as she pushed a long strand of her wavy wheat-colored hair from her sky blue eyes. "An angel dream. Now, that's important."

The red digital numbers on her clock said it was three twenty-eight in the morning. But Christina was somehow fully awake. She turned on her bedside lamp, then pulled a fabric-covered notebook from under her pillow.

Her dream journal. Tenderly she ran her hands across its tapestry floral-print cover. She'd found this blank, lined, slightly faded book last month at the Pine Ridge Middle School flea market. She'd snapped it up right away, as if it had somehow called to her. For only a dollar, she'd purchased a book just perfect for recording her dreams, something she'd been wanting to do for a long time.

Opening the book, she pressed its smooth, slightly yellowed pages down flat. Christina believed in the importance of dreams. They spoke to a person in an extraordinary way. And by writing them in a book, she learned about herself—what her deepest, innermost thoughts and feelings really were.

But dreams of angels were different, she believed. She wasn't sure exactly how they differed from more everyday dreams, but she believed they were important. After all, an angel spoke of the deep mysteries of this world and other worlds. What symbol could be more important than that?

Christina even considered the idea—though she might not freely admit it for fear of seeming foolish and overly imaginative—that the angels in dreams were more than symbols. Maybe angels really came into dreams, were actually there, for some crucial reason.

With the black felt-tipped pen she kept by her bedside, she began to write.

Tonight I had an awesome dream, she wrote in her large, loopy handwriting. *I dreamed I was lost in the dark. It was terrifying.* She set down the rest of the dream as best she could remember. Ever since she'd started keeping a nightly journal of her dreams a month ago, she'd found them easier and easier to remember.

> And on the other side of the doorway stood the most beautiful angel I've ever seen. The light coming from her was nearly blinding. Her face was so full of love that all my fear vanished. But what did she want to tell me? Why was she there?

Christina put her pen down and considered the question. Lately she'd thought about angels a lot. She had reason to. For one thing, she knew where they lived. At least where three of them lived.

The Angels Crossing Bridge stood silently spanning a rushing creek, deep in the Pine Manor woods. That was where she and her two friends Ashley and Katie had first encountered angels. Later, their friend Molly had seen an angel there, too. Since that time, their lives had been touched by angels in amazing ways.

Was it just a matter of having actually seen the angels?

Christina thought it was. Once they'd seen the angels—once their eyes had been opened to the real existence of angels—they could always see them, and they felt their celestial presence everywhere.

Christina picked up her pen and continued writing.

> This month, my horoscope says big changes are in store for me. I wonder what they could be. June is nearly over and nothing here at the ranch seems about to change. Daisy had her

colt in the middle of the month. It was exciting, but I don't think it counts as a big change. School ended for summer break last week, which is a change but not a huge one. Unless something unexpected happens by the end of next week, my horoscope will be wrong. That happens sometimes, I guess. Astrologers can make mistakes, like anyone.

Christina had complete faith in the power of the stars to foretell the future. She did realize, though, that the art of astrology involved reading the signs correctly. Mistakes could be made. Still, she thought Ruth Elliot, who wrote the column in *The Pine Ridge Courier*, usually did a good job.

With a yawn, she leaned back against her pillow. Maybe the change would be the new volunteer program at the hospital. She'd signed up to visit with sick children staying at Children's House, a very large old green Victorian house donated to the Pine Ridge Hospital Center last year. After six months of renovation, it had opened and was used for young patients staying in the hospital for more than a week—so their hospital time would be more homey and comfortable. Christina had volunteered to go and keep at least one kid company each week.

"That must be the change," she said, yawning again. Her eyes suddenly heavy, she closed her dream journal and turned off her bedroom lamp.

This time her sleep was peaceful and dreamless.

* * *

In the morning, a wide shaft of buttery sunshine poured through the window onto her face. Throwing off her blanket, Christina swung her long legs out of bed and stood barefoot in her bedroom. The cabin she and her mother lived in on the grounds of the Pine Manor Ranch had a rustic look, from its stone fireplace in the living room to the furniture, pillows, earth-colored rugs, and low, rough-hewn beamed ceilings in every room.

She pulled on jeans, a white peasant-style blouse, and tan boots, which came up to her knees. Quickly, she did her thick hair up in a single, long, loose braid. The image in her mirror showed a tall, naturally pretty girl, dressed for comfort and movement. The tiny white scar that cut across her left eyebrow—the remains of a riding fall when she was little—was the only thing marring the perfect smoothness of her skin.

"Christina! Are you awake?"

She knew the voice outside her door well. "Come on in, Ashley," she called.

A petite girl with a wash of light freckles across her delicate-featured face stuck her head in the door. "Oh, good, you're dressed and everything." Her riotous red curls were somewhat controlled by an emerald green cloth headband that matched her eyes. "Come on," she said. "I have to take up the back end of a trail ride and I want company."

"Okay," Christina agreed.

Christina grabbed a whole-wheat doughnut from the bread box on the counter in the kitchen, then headed out the front door with Ashley. They walked up the dirt road leading toward the rust red stable on the right and

Ashley's pale yellow ranch-style house on the left. "I dreamed about an angel last night," Christina confided.

"Oh, wow," Ashley said, impressed. "Do you think it means something?"

Christina nodded. "Definitely." She appreciated that Ashley took her seriously. They'd grown up together on the horse ranch that Ashley's parents owned, more like sisters than mere best friends. Even though Ashley didn't share Christina's fascination with dreams and other mystical things, she kept an open mind. She never mocked, and she set store by Christina's dreams and premonitions.

"Do you have a feeling about it?" Ashley asked. "I mean one of your *feelings*?"

Christina thought about it. "Yes, I think I do." She knew Ashley was referring to the touch of ESP she sometimes seemed to possess. When Christina had a feeling about something, it was often right. Her special feelings only concerned small things—like if someone was about to show up unexpectedly, or if the phone was about to ring, or where something lost might be found. Yet it happened often enough that Christina had come to rely on her premonitions to guide her.

"What do you think it means?" Ashley asked.

"I'm not sure," Christina admitted. "But I'd like to go to the bridge today," she said. "Something tells me I should."

"I'll go with you after this trail ride is over," Ashley offered. "Katie and Molly are coming over then. We can all go together."

"Great," Christina said as they reached the stable.

Jeremy and Jason, Ashley's lanky, red-haired seventeen-year-old twin brothers, were already on horseback. Other riders, six paying guests at the ranch, sat in their saddles, waiting.

"Come on, Ashley, hurry up, everybody's waiting for you," Jason barked impatiently.

"Hold your horses," Ashley told him. She smiled at Christina. "Hold your *horses*, get it?"

"Got it," Christina said, rolling her eyes at Ashley's corniness, but smiling just the same. The girls went into the stable and saddled two brown mares. Ashley chose Daisy, and Christina was glad to see that her favorite horse, Bridey, was still available. Some people found Bridey skittish and difficult, but she and Christina had an unspoken understanding. Christina respected Bridey's proud nature and Bridey seemed to know that. In return, she handled beautifully for Christina.

The girls walked the horses out of the stable and mounted them. Making a quick, sharp clicking sound, Jeremy signaled the horses to start moving. He headed the group toward the thick pinewoods that ringed the ranch. The ancient woods were crisscrossed with horse trails artificially etched into the deep pine-needle carpet by the repeated pounding of horse hooves over the same paths time and again.

Normally, Christina would have relished a morning ride on a gorgeous, balmy early summer's day, but today she was restless. Entering the woods and breathing in the deep, moist, pine-laden air only made her more eager to get to the Angels Crossing Bridge. Impatient for some clue as to the meaning of her dream, she felt that perhaps an answer awaited her at the bridge.

Another feeling had also started growing within her—the feeling that maybe her horoscope was right after all.

Something was about to change. She didn't know what. But her skin tingled with anticipation. Every nerve felt alert. And the angels were somehow involved.

3

"I don't feel like going to the bridge right now," Molly Morgan complained as she hung on a section of the split-rail fence that penned off the corral next to the stable. "I wanted to ride." The V-shaped silver tip of her polished black riding boots glistened in the sunlight as she gave the wooden fence a petulant kick.

"Aw, come on," Christina coaxed. "I need to go. We can ride when we get back."

Molly gathered her long, straight white-blond hair and twisted it into a coil, as if thinking about what she really wanted to do. "Why can't we ride there?"

"All the horses are out on trail rides or they're being used for lessons right now, and I don't want to wait," Christina explained.

Just then, the leather satchel at Molly's feet began ringing. "What now?" she sighed, rolling her blue-green eyes skyward. Rummaging in the bag, she lifted out a slim black cordless phone and flipped it open. "Hello, Mother. Yes, hi, Mom . . . Yeah . . . The limo service is fine. . . . No problem. But not until six o'clock, okay? Yes, I'll eat lunch. I promise . . . I *said* I promise! All right. Thanks. Bye."

Closing her phone, Molly threw her head back and let out a frustrated cry. "She's driving me crazy!" she shouted.

"Your mom?" Christina questioned.

"Yes! Lately, she's calling me every second. Every mealtime she calls and reminds me to eat!"

"She's just worried because of your . . . condition."

"I'm not anorexic anymore!" Molly cried. "Look at me. I'm fat!"

"Not quite," Christina disagreed with a stern scowl. Her friend was as slim as a fashion model, and as pretty as one, too. The fact that she called herself fat worried Christina. It was a sign that she still wasn't looking at herself realistically.

Molly did look *much* better than she had looked a few months ago, though. Back then, her anorexia—the emotional disorder that made her try to starve herself into a state of life-threatening thinness—had a deadly hold on her. Molly's thinness and malnutrition had landed her in the hospital more than once. But lately, Molly seemed to be winning the battle to get well. Although still thin, she'd lost the gaunt, starved look she'd had when the disease held her tight.

"I wonder why your mother is extra worried about you now?" Christina said. "You know, since everything's going so well with you."

"I'm not sure. Maybe she'd just rather think about me instead of about Dad."

"What do you mean?"

"She and Dad have been arguing a lot. It started ever since Dad quit his job and decided to become a painter. I don't think Mom is used to having him around the house so much."

Christina nodded though she couldn't really imagine what that would be like. Her own father had abandoned her and her mother when she was very small. Christina didn't remember much about him. As far back as she could recall, it had always been just her and her mother, Alice, who worked as a riding instructor and ranch hand here at the ranch.

A slamming door made Christina turn and look across the road. Ashley was coming down her front-porch steps. Ashley's golden retriever, Champ, walked between Ashley and a tall, auburn-haired girl wearing a baseball cap with its brim turned backward. The girl smiled and waved at Molly and Christina.

"Hi, Katie," Christina called and waved to her.

With her knowing attitude and slightly swaggering walk, Katie Nelson still seemed to Christina like a city girl, even though she'd been living in Pine Ridge with her aunt and uncle—following the terrible death of her parents in a car accident—for nearly a year now. "You guys ready to go?" Katie asked in her usual direct manner as she and Ashley approached Christina and Molly.

"Oh, all right," Molly gave in. "These boots aren't really comfortable to walk in, though."

"Would you like us to carry you?" Katie asked with an amused twinkle in her amber eyes. "Come on. You'll survive."

With Champ frisking at their side, they walked behind the back of the stable to a spot where the thick trees parted slightly, making a natural doorway into the woods. A warm breeze rustled the pines, sounding like invisible wood sprites calling to them, whispering. Champ barked at the woods, then looked at the girls, his tail wagging. "Okay, Champ, we're going," Ashley said with a light laugh. Together, the girls walked forward, entering the woods.

Christina drank in the rich pine smell. She was always struck by the oldness of the woods, its ancient energy. She sensed that the thick, abundant pines sent out a life force so strong she could feel it in the same way she felt a breeze, or a ripple in a stream. "I'm always happy here in the woods," she told her friends as they padded along on the thick carpet of fallen pine needles. "I think these trees give off energy that gets into me somehow. I feel stronger after leaving."

"I feel the same way," Katie agreed. "But I don't think it's because the trees are zapping me with super energy."

"Why do you think it is, then?" Ashley asked, as open-minded to Katie's strictly rational thought as she was to Christina's metaphysical musings.

Katie shrugged. "It's just the peace and quiet. It calms you down."

"Thanks for reminding me," Molly said, abruptly setting her leather bag down next to a rock. "If that phone rang here in the woods, I think I'd go crazy. I'll pick it up on the way back."

"I don't think it would ring," Christina said. "The energy here in the woods would block it out somehow."

They continued along without talking. Champ ran ahead playfully and then ran back. His occasional barking was the only noise they heard until the babble of water called to them, orienting them. It was easy to get lost in the vast woods, but the narrow, winding stream off to their right told them they were headed in the right direction.

They followed the path of the stream until it seemed to disappear into the side of a hill. They climbed the hill to its crest. "There it is," Ashley said softly.

They all gazed down at the covered bridge spanning a wide, rock-strewn, rushing creek. The spraying, splashing creek created a break in the woods where— since no trees grew there—a line of sunshine made its way in as if a brilliant beacon were slicing a path through the woods. It danced on the water that cascaded down small, rocky inclines, sending up sprays of bright foam, and glinted off the shingled roof of the cracked and faded wooden bridge. Some light filtered down onto the bridge between the cracks where heavy beam bracings supported the roof. The shadowy old planking on the floor was dappled with light from above.

"Hey, look!" Katie cried. "There are some people on the bridge!"

The girls broke into a run, hurrying down the hill, Champ plunging on ahead of them. Christina quickly saw what Katie had seen.

Three people stood on the bridge. She knew who they were—Norma, Edwina, and Ned.

The girls had met them on or near this bridge before. The three claimed to be angels, and Christina believed them. Absolutely. Although they were definitely eccentric, Christina loved the warm feeling she had whenever she met them.

The girls and Champ clattered onto the wooden bridge and then stopped, taking in the sight in front of them.

Tall, broad-shouldered Ned wore a very formal black business suit. His soft face, which always reminded Christina of the man in the moon, wore a serious expression. His shocking lavender-blue eyes were narrowed in concentration. He stood next to a blackboard and pointed with a long pointer at various symbols written on the board.

The two women sat on metal folding chairs, facing Ned and his blackboard. Norma, a woman with strong, angular features, was dressed in a very tailored red business suit. Her thick black hair was pulled back in a fat French braid.

Beside her sat a beautiful woman with a fashion model's classic good looks. Edwina's blond curls fell softly to her shoulders, cascading past the bow of her white blouse. Both women had the same startling lavender-blue eyes as Ned.

"What are they doing?" Ashley asked.

"It looks like they're having a business meeting," Molly observed.

Ned noticed the girls standing there and smiled. "Our friends!" he greeted, his eyes shining with sincere welcome. The two women turned and smiled. "Come," he said. "Have a seat while we finish up our meeting."

The girls stepped forward. Ned gestured toward four empty folding chairs behind Norma and Edwina. "These chairs weren't here a minute ago," Katie whispered as they sat down.

"That's angels for you," Christina said softly, and Champ settled down contentedly beside them.

"As I was saying," Ned said, resuming his serious attitude, "we'll encourage those boys to steal Mr. Johnson's car at about seven o'clock."

"Great idea," said Norma, writing something down on a long yellow pad. "We can each take one boy and whisper in his ear."

"Wait a minute," Katie said, raising her hand. "Wait a minute!"

Ned nodded at her. "Yes?"

Katie stood, as if she were in school. "I thought you three were supposed to be angels."

"We are," Ned said.

"And you're encouraging some kids to steal someone's car?" Katie cried incredulously. "That's not exactly my idea of what angels do."

Edwina laughed lightly, her laughter floating on the air like wind chimes. "Oh, yes, I see how that could possibly be confusing."

"Just slightly," Katie said with an ironic smile.

"You see, Katie, the boys are going to steal Mr. Johnson's car because he's had too many beers with supper, and we don't want him to get behind the wheel of his car. He might hurt himself or someone else. This way we'll take a cab home."

"We?" Molly questioned.

"Oh, yes," Norma continued. "I'll be in the cab with him. I'll whisper to the driver to turn down a road where there's been a car accident. It will make Mr. Johnson see that the accident could have been his. We hope he'll go home and think about how he drinks and drives. We hope he'll stop."

"What if he doesn't stop?" Ashley asked.

"Then he'll probably have a car accident eventually," Ned said sadly. "We can't force him not to drink so much. Well, I suppose, strictly speaking, we could—I mean, we have the power to—but it's not the angel way."

"What about the boys?" Molly asked. "You're encouraging them to do something bad, aren't you?"

"Those three have been doing bad things all this year," Ned said with a wave of his hand. "We're trying to get them to straighten out before it's too late."

"You're straightening them out by encouraging them to steal a car?" Katie asked skeptically. "Excuse me, but I don't get it."

"They're going to get stuck on a one-lane road behind an Officer Winger," Edwina explained with indulgent patience. She looked to Norma. "Remind me to contact an Officer Winger today. We'll need to reserve one."

Norma wrote on her pad. "Reserve an Officer Winger," she murmured as she wrote.

"We've met Officer Winger," Ashley spoke up. "Is there more than one of them? I think I've met several."

Christina leaned forward in her chair and listened intently. She was very curious about these strange police officers they'd started encountering ever since becoming aware of the angels.

"Yes, there are a lot of them," Norma said. "We're very proud of our Officer Winger program. In fact, there will soon be more. We're due to attend a graduation at the Winger Academy today. A whole new graduating class of cadets will be released into the world."

"Now, to return to discussing our plan," Ned said. "The boys will be stuck behind the Officer Winger and become quite nervous. After they've had enough time to panic and think about what will happen to them if they're caught with a stolen car, Officer Winger will pull them over. He'll pretend to write them a ticket for a broken turn signal, but when the boys read the ticket, it will be a piece of paper with the words 'Return the Car' written on it. In a panic, they'll drive back to Joe's Tavern, return the car, and be so shook up, they'll never steal anything again. We hope."

"Hey, brilliant plan!" Katie cried. "You guys are good at this."

"What if all the Wingers are busy?" Edwina questioned. "A lot of them will be at the graduation."

"I'll do it then," Ned replied. "I have some Winger training."

"Very good," Norma said. "Should we discuss the plan for assisting the runaway slaves on the underground railroad next?"

"If you like," said Ned. "I was thinking that you could pose as a Native American guide and take one of Harriet Tubman's groups safely through the woods so she can go back and get another group. That way, the young woman who's worried about getting her sick daughter safely through won't back out and be subjected to a lifetime of slavery."

"Sounds good," Norma agreed. "Seeing Harriet there

will give her the confidence she needs to make the escape."

"Hold it!" Katie cried. "Harriet Tubman? *The* Harriet Tubman who helped slaves escape to freedom? Is that who you're talking about?"

"Of course," Edwina said sweetly.

"She lived over a hundred years ago!" Katie shouted.

Christina smiled quietly. Things like this, which defied rational explanation, really got to Katie.

"Wonderful woman," Edwina commented fondly. "So brave. People like her make our work easy. Harriet is practically an angel herself, an earth angel to be sure."

"Does that mean you guys can travel through time?" Katie questioned, narrowing her sharp eyes skeptically.

Christina sat even further forward, eager to hear the answer. She strongly suspected they could travel through time, but she wanted to hear them say so for certain.

"Ah, time," Norma sighed. "Time is such an earthly notion."

"Well, this *is* earth," Katie reminded her a bit impatiently.

Christina cringed at Katie's disrespect. These were angels, after all.

"Yes, we move through time," Edwina replied warmly.

"What's the future going to be like?" Molly asked excitedly.

"We can't tell you," Norma said. "That's in our rule book—rule number three thousand and twelve." Suddenly, the thick black watch on her wrist beeped loudly. Norma checked it and her eyes went wide. "Oh, my, we're going to be late for the graduation. We'd better go."

As Ned and Norma busied themselves with folding their notebooks and wheeling the blackboard off the bridge, Edwina turned to Molly. "The future is lovely, dear. You'll like it a lot. You, especially."

"Me?" Molly gasped.

"Yes. You've picked the best career for the future."

"Do you mean because I want to be an astronaut?" Molly asked.

"Absolutely. You stay with that plan. Let me tell you, you wouldn't believe some of the things that are going to happen. I've seen it and it's just so—"

"Edwina!" Norma called sternly from the far side of the bridge where she waited with Ned. She gave Edwina a serious look, a look which said, 'Be quiet, you're not supposed to tell that.'"

"Sorry," Edwina said, covering her mouth, her eyes lit mischievously.

"The Wingers are waiting!" Ned reminded her brightly.

"Coming!" Edwina said. "Bye, girls!" She turned to join Ned and Norma.

"Wait!" Christina cried, jumping to her feet as she suddenly remembered her dream. "I have to ask you about . . ." Her voice trailed off as the angelic threesome walked off briskly, disappearing from view sooner than seemed natural.

"They sure do come and go quickly," Katie commented wryly.

"I didn't get to ask about my dream," Christina complained, slumping into the folding chair. "I need to know why there was an angel in it."

"I know," Molly said. "Maybe it was a premonition. Your ESP was telling you that you'd see angels. And you did—right here and now on the bridge. I bet that was it."

"Could be," Christina said, considering it. Molly's reasoning made sense. Yet, somehow, she thought there was more to the dream. Something bigger.

Ashley walked to the far end of the bridge and looked both ways. "Where did that blackboard go?" she asked, turning back to her friends. "It just disappeared."

"That's angels for you," Christina said.

The girls and Champ walked off the bridge back the way they'd come. When Christina looked back over her shoulder, the folding chairs were also gone. She noticed Katie staring at the now empty bridge, too. Their eyes met. Katie scowled and Christina grinned.

They headed back up the hill, away from the bridge, and for a while, they didn't talk much. Christina was thinking about the angelic meeting she'd just witnessed.

It was odd, the way the angels worked in such a roundabout manner. She found comfort in it, liking the idea that things didn't simply happen for no reason. The idea that someone, somewhere, had a plan for things— that there was a meaning to all the seemingly senseless things that happened in the world—gave her a good feeling.

After a while, her mind wandered off the angels and back to her horoscope. She started to wonder what big change was in store for her. Thinking of this reminded her that she was about to start working at the new Children's House. "I start at Children's House this

Saturday," she said, breaking the silence.

"Do you mean that big old house behind the hospital?" Ashley asked.

Christina nodded. "That's the one. They still need more volunteers. Why don't the three of you do it with me?"

"I could probably do it with you," Katie said.

"I can't," Ashley said. "They need me here to take out trail rides and help your mom in the stables. Any free time I have after that goes to Dr. Jeffers." Ashley had a part-time job assisting the veterinarian who looked after the horses on the ranch. She hoped to be a veterinarian herself, when she was older.

"I can't, either," Molly said. "I'm going to Space Camp in Florida at the end of the month. I can't wait. Did you hear what Edwina said to me, about space? How did she know I want to be an astronaut?"

"She's probably watching you," Christina suggested.

"That's a nice idea," Molly said with a small smile. "I hope you're right about that."

"Me too. But I know one thing I was *wrong* about," Christina said.

"What's that?" Molly asked.

"I was wrong about your phone not working here in the woods. Listen." The girls stopped, and sure enough, an insistent ringing was coming from Molly's bag, still leaning against a rock several yards ahead.

Molly sighed and rolled her eyes. "It's just Mom wanting to know if I ate my lunch."

"And you didn't," Ashley pointed out. "Let's go back to my house. I'll make sandwiches."

When they reached the leather bag, Molly reached in and picked out the phone. "Ashley's making lunch now," she said.

She answered a series of questions from her mother before hanging up. Molly faced her friends. "Do you think cellular phones work in outer space?" she asked.

"I don't know," Katie replied. Christina and Ashley shrugged.

"I sure hope not," Molly said with a sigh as they headed out of the woods. "I sure hope not."

4

"This is great for the kids," Katie said that Saturday as Christina and she walked up the long pathway to the huge Victorian house in front of them. The house was four stories high, with several gabled rooftops. An open porch wrapped around the entire bottom floor. Though the house was old, it had been freshly painted green with bright blue shutters, making it a cheerful, welcoming place.

"If I were sick I'd much rather be here than in a regular hospital," Christina agreed.

When they walked into the wide front hallway, Christina quickly saw that this was—despite its homey appearance—still very much a hospital. A nurse sat at a broad desk. And there was a hospital smell in the air, a combination of antiseptic and medicine smells. "Can I help you girls?" the front-desk nurse asked pleasantly.

Christina explained that they were volunteers, and the nurse directed them up the steps to the second floor, telling them to see Ms. Baker, who was in charge of volunteers. They found Ms. Baker, a friendly woman with short gray and white hair, sitting in her office, which had probably once been a bedroom of the house. "Come on, girls," she said, getting up from her desk. "I'll introduce you to some of the kids."

They followed her into a sunny room with yellow walls and white lace curtains. Four hospital beds faced one another. Two of the beds were empty. In another, a blond girl of about eleven with glasses sat reading a Nancy Drew book. In the fourth sat a girl of about seven with chin-length brown hair and large brown eyes. Ms. Baker introduced the older girl as Beth and the younger one as Marta. "Just keep the girls company," Ms. Baker told Christina and Katie as she headed out of the room. "The days really get long in here for them."

"Hey, cool, Nancy Drew," Katie said, approaching Beth's bed. "I love her. Which one are you reading?"

"*The Double Horror of Fenley Place*," Beth replied.

Katie perched on the edge of Beth's bed. "I haven't read that one. What kind of mess has Nancy gotten herself into this time?"

As Beth began recounting the plot to Katie, Christina approached the younger girl. "Hi, Marta," she said. "How are you feeling today?"

"Okay," Marta replied as if to brush Christina off. Christina studied her expression. It was hard to read. Her eyes laughed as if she wanted to share a joke, yet she didn't make direct eye contact, like she was hiding something.

"What do you like to do?" Christina asked. "Would you

like me to get crayons or a puzzle book or something? I saw some downstairs on a table."

"No thanks," Marta replied.

"Is there anything you'd like to do?"

Marta shook her head. "Maybe you should go visit another kid."

Christina was unsure what to say next. Surely this little girl must want some company. She had to be lonely and frightened here. Yet she seemed happy.

As Christina puzzled over this, the answer appeared. The head of a small, furry black kitten wriggled its way out from behind Marta's pillow. Christina smiled and scooped him up. "Hey there, cutie," she whispered to the kitten.

At once, a frantic expression came into Marta's dark eyes. She clutched Christina's arm. "Don't tell, please," she begged in an urgent whisper. "Nurse Worly will put him out. She will."

"Who is Nurse Worly?" Christina asked.

"She's the head nurse. She's very strict, and there are no pets allowed."

Guiltily, Christina checked the door for any sign of this nurse. Then she turned her back to it, to hide the fact that she held a squirming kitten. "Where did you get him?"

"He came to the window two nights ago," Marta told her. "It was raining out, really hard, and he was crying, so I let him in. Isn't he cute? He's so little."

"He must have climbed up onto the roof from a tree," Christina guessed, scratching the kitten between the ears.

"No, he was born here," Marta said. "Ms. Baker told us a stray cat got into the attic through a small hole in the roof and had kittens. The hospital people thought they brought them all down, but they must have missed Raindrop."

"That's what you named him?"

"He was so wet he looked like one big raindrop," Marta told her. "I feed him from my tray at mealtime, and he's been sleeping with me at night."

No wonder Marta didn't seem lonely and miserable, Christina considered. She had a little friend with her. But how would she feel when he was discovered? "You can't hide him forever, you know," Christina pointed out delicately.

"Yes, I can," Marta insisted. "Why not?"

"Does Beth know about him?" Christina asked in a whisper.

"She knows," Marta said. "But she won't tell. All she wants to do is read, but she's not mean or anything."

Christina nodded, but she still didn't see how Marta could hide this kitten forever. "What if I find you a box?" she suggested. "Then maybe you could at least hide him in the closet there next to your bed when someone like Nurse Worly is around."

"That's a good idea," Marta agreed. "Sometimes I see empty boxes out in the hall."

"I'll be right back," Christina said, handing the kitten back to Marta. Then she left the room in search of a box. As soon as she stepped out, she saw a small pile of about three cardboard boxes. As she bent to pick one up, she sensed someone coming up behind her.

"Hi, Christina," said a boy.

Christina turned and gasped lightly. "Hi, Matt."

Matt Larson was Molly's boyfriend. He was also the only boy Christina had ever had a serious crush on. She tried to forget about it, out of loyalty to Molly, but whenever she saw Matt, her heartbeat quickened.

He was tall with strong, handsome features and long, thick brown hair. In Christina's opinion, even his wire-rim glasses were a plus. They made him look intelligent. But it was more than just his looks. Whenever he and Christina talked, they seemed to have so much in common. Matt even told her once that he believed in angels.

"What are you doing here?" she asked him.

"I volunteered to hang out with some kids who are stuck here for a while. They're down the hall over there," he said, pointing behind himself.

"Wow. Me too," Christina said. She looked at him and smiled. He smiled back. Then Christina thought of Molly and a guilty feeling washed over her. "So," she said. "Molly leaves for space camp soon. That's exciting, isn't it?"

"I'm really happy for her," he said. "For a while it looked like her parents weren't going to let her go. I'm glad they changed their minds."

"Yeah," Christina agreed. "She's much better with her sickness and all. I'm glad they realized that."

Matt nodded. He looked as if he were about to say something, but didn't. "I'd better get back to my little guys," he said. "So long. I guess I'll see you here again."

"Guess so," Christina said with a nervous laugh. "Bye."

Her heart still pounding, Christina grabbed a box and hurried back to Marta. "What took so long?" Marta asked, cradling Raindrop in her arms. "Your face is all red. Are you okay?"

Christina's hands flew to her cheeks. Marta was right. They were red hot! How mortifying!

"How is everything?" came a gentle voice behind Christina.

Still flushed and embarrassed, Christina turned to see a short, attractive East Indian woman with long black hair. The white coat she wore over her simple blue dress and the stethoscope around her neck identified her as a doctor.

"Doctor Sebruch," Marta cried happily. She placed her hand over a lump under the covers beside her. Christina bit lightly on her lip. Surely the doctor had to notice the moving lump.

5

Christina kept her eyes on Dr. Sebruch. Hadn't she noticed the moving lump? Or was she simply ignoring it? Christina tensed as she waited for the doctor's response. She hated the idea that she might discover the kitten and take him away. She liked Marta and didn't want to see the little girl disappointed.

Dr. Sebruch brushed the top of Marta's hair. "How is my little Marta today?" she asked in a soft voice rich with a warm Indian accent. She opened her hand to reveal five round lavender crystal stones. "I brought you these."

Marta slipped her hand out from under the cover and, cupping her two hands together, eagerly received the stones. "Thank you. They're so beautiful." She turned to Christina. "I collect rocks," she explained. "Aren't these great?"

"Very beautiful," Christina agreed. "They're crystals, too. Some people think crystals direct good energy to you."

Dr. Sebruch nodded. "Lavender crystals are thought to have healing properties," she added.

Christina smiled at her. So often people didn't believe in the power of crystals. She was happy to find an adult who did, especially a doctor.

A little mewing sound came from under the covers.

Christina froze. She and Marta exchanged darting, anxious glances.

Dr. Sebruch had to have heard the kitten, but she gave no indication of it. "If you'll excuse me, girls, I'll go say hello to our dear Beth," she said. "Have a good day."

Christina's shoulders collapsed with relief. Marta smiled and leaned back in her pillow.

As Dr. Sebruch walked across the room to Beth, Christina stepped between the doctor and Marta. The girl lifted her kitten from under the blanket. "That was close," Christina whispered.

Dr. Sebruch left the room five minutes later. The moment she was gone, Christina found a towel and put it in the box for Raindrop. She gently dropped the kitten into the box. "There," she said. "Now he has a proper place to sleep."

"He sleeps with me," Marta insisted.

"But what if he wanders away while you're asleep?"

"He won't," Marta said, lifting Raindrop from the box. "How do you know?"

"Raindrop loves me," Marta stated simply. "So I know."

Christina didn't have the heart to argue this point. "Okay," she said. "But there's the box for him if you need it."

As she spoke, a large nurse with very dark hair and

very pale skin came into the room. "Nurse Worly," Marta whispered fiercely. Christina stepped in front of Raindrop. With her hands behind her back, she wriggled her fingers, indicating that Marta should pass her the kitten. She did, and, with the kitten still behind her, Christina backed up against the wall.

Nurse Worly clapped her hands. "All right now. Volunteer time is over. These girls need their rest."

"But we just got here," Katie protested.

"Come earlier next time," Nurse Worly said curtly. "This is nap time." As the nurse crossed the room and busied herself straightening Beth's covers, Christina opened the closet door and set Raindrop down. She winked at Marta, who smiled back, her hand concealing her grin.

"Bye, Beth," Katie said, heading for the door. "I'll bring you some more Nancys next time I come."

"Cool. Thanks," said Beth.

Christina waved good-bye to Marta and joined Katie at the door. Together, they walked down the stairs and out the front door. "That was fun," Katie said when they stepped onto the outside porch.

"It was," Christina agreed. "Marta is hiding a kitten."

"I know. Beth told me. I hope she doesn't get caught."

"It would really upset her to lose him," Christina said. "It must be awful to be stuck in a hospital, even a nice one like this."

"What's wrong with Marta?" Katie asked.

"You know, I forgot to ask. Or maybe I didn't forget. Maybe I just didn't want to bring up an unpleasant subject right away. Why is Beth there?"

"They're running tests on her to find out why she keeps getting headaches."

Christina nodded. "I hope it's nothing serious. Guess who's also a volunteer? Matt Larson."

"Cool. I'm surprised Molly didn't say anything about it. I wonder if she even knows," Katie said.

"Those two don't really talk all that much, do they?" Christina said. "Molly doesn't seem all that interested in him sometimes."

"Well, they've been going together awhile, I think. But you're right, they don't seem madly in love or anything. Are you still interested in him?"

Leave it to Katie to get right to the point. Christina sighed. "Let's just say I wish he wasn't seeing Molly," she admitted.

"I thought so," Katie said. "You two do seem to have more in common than he and Molly do. You're both interested in . . . you know . . . flaky stuff."

"Flaky stuff!" Christina cried indignantly.

"Yeah. No offense, but you know. Crystals, horoscopes, tarot cards and all. Didn't you tell me he was interested in UFOs?"

"None of that is flaky," Christina argued. "After everything we've seen, everything that's happened, how can you still be so close-minded?"

"I'm not close-minded," Katie cried. "I just happen to believe in things I can see and understand—things that make sense!"

"What about angels?" Christina challenged.

"I've *seen* the angels," Katie replied. "I see them so I believe in them. Simple."

"But maybe there are other ways of seeing," Christina countered.

"Now you're getting flaky," Katie said.

"No, I'm not. What about dreams? Dreams are another way of seeing. You don't see dreams with your eyes. Everyone dreams. You can't say you don't believe in it."

"All right. Everyone dreams, but I don't think dreams give us messages or anything like that."

"You don't?"

"No."

"What about ESP? That's another way of seeing," Christina pressed.

"I don't believe in ESP," Katie said firmly as they left the path and crossed in front of the large main building of the Pine Ridge Hospital. "I think people who are very sensitive and alert put little clues together, clues that other people might miss. From all these little clues, they make a good guess about what's going to happen."

"I suppose that's a possible explanation," Christina admitted. "But that's not how it feels when it happens to me."

They had reached the bus stop. Christina put her hands on her forehead and clenched her eyes shut. "I know that the bus is about to turn the corner, right now. Here it comes. I sense it coming!" Christina opened her eyes and smiled triumphantly. The bus had just come around the corner and was heading toward them.

"Awesome," Katie murmured, her amber eyes riveted to the approaching bus. "How did you do that?"

"I tuned in to the cosmic vibes given out by the bus," Christina said with great seriousness. "I felt the spirit of the bus driver and the passengers as they drew nearer and nearer."

"Really?" Katie questioned as the bus pulled to a stop in front of them and the doors opened. "That really is amazing."

"I also read this little sign here," Christina said with a mischievous twinkle in her eyes as she tapped the metal plate posted on the bus stop sign. "It's a bus timetable. It helps."

"Oh, you rat!" Katie cried.

Laughing, Christina danced up onto the bus. "Gotcha!" she cried gleefully. "Gotcha good!"

6

Dear Dream Journal—Tonight I dreamed I heard a banging sound outside my window. In my dream, I got out of bed to look and discovered a bat banging up against the glass. Its wings flapped hard against the panes, as if it wanted to get in.

It frightened me and I ran to get Mom. But before I could reach the door, the bat crashed through the window. Glass shattered everywhere. The bat flew all around me, shrieking. In my dream I screamed so loudly that I must have awakened myself.

It was a terrible dream. Horrible!

I'm writing it now here in bed, but I'm still trembling a little. Is this bat the thing that I sense is coming toward me? Is it something scary, or bad? I sure hope not.

*   *   *

Christina closed her dream journal and got out of bed. She went to her dresser and took some white crystal stones from the top drawer. She'd found them in the stream in the Pine Manor woods.

Clutching one crystal in the palm of each hand, she sat on the floor and inhaled deeply. Then, exhaling in a slow whoosh of air, she began to chant, her voice low and deep.

"Ohhhmmmmm." And again. "Ohmmmmm."

If something bad was coming her way, she was going to surround herself with good energy. The crystals would help to draw positive energy to her. This was something she firmly believed. The chanting would help her meditate. Meditating cleared her mind and helped her think more clearly afterward. It would keep her centered and strong. She would be ready to meet whatever was coming and, hopefully, turn it back.

The gentle creak of Christina's door opening made her eyes shoot open.

Her mother stood in the doorway, tall, barefoot, and wearing a simple white cotton nightgown. Alice Kramer's chin-length blond hair was tousled from sleep. "Christina, why are you awake?" she asked sleepily.

"Sorry, Mom. Did I wake you?"

Alice rubbed her eyes. "I'm not sure. I just woke up and felt like checking on you."

Goosebumps formed on Christina's arms. Her mother felt it, too. Something was coming.

"I had a bad dream," Christina confided. "It scared me. I dreamed a bat crashed through the window." As she spoke she started to shake. Her voice quivered slightly.

Alice stepped into the room and knelt next to Christina, rubbing her shoulders soothingly. "You're shaking. It really upset you, didn't it?"

Christina nodded.

"What are you doing on the floor?"

"The dream made me think something bad was coming. I'm trying to keep it away by meditating," Christina explained.

"Nothing bad is coming," Alice said, tightening her hold on Christina.

"But what if it is?" Christina opened her hands to show the crystals she clutched. "I didn't know what else to do."

"I see," Alice said seriously. "You have the crystals because you're trying to bring good energy to yourself. Is that it?"

"Yes." Christina knew her mother understood. They shared a lot of the same beliefs in mystical things.

Alice had first introduced Christina to the idea that there was energy in the universe that flowed in ways people didn't yet understand. She was the one who told Christina that she sensed the woods held strange yet good power spots, although she didn't believe in angels.

"Okay. I'll meditate with you," Alice said in a quiet and serious tone. She took one of Christina's crystals and wrapped her strong, wide hand around it. Sitting cross-legged next to Christina, she breathed deeply.

Christina drew breath in time with her mother's. Together, they let their breath out as they chanted. "Ohmmmmm."

The vibration of Christina's own voice tingled in her breastbone and in the bones of her face. The chanting calmed her fears as her voice mingled with her mother's slightly lower voice.

"Ohmmmmm."

She felt very close to her mother. It was as if their mingled voices created one voice, one energy. Together, nothing bad could get them. Together with her mother, Christina felt stronger than any bad thing that might try to crash into her world.

7

Christina and Katie visited the hospital again on Wednesday. "I hope Beth likes these Nancys," Katie said, balancing ten hardcover Nancy Drew mysteries in her arms. "They're the old ones, you know, from the 1930s and 40s. They were Aunt Rainie's. I found them in the barn. I think the old ones are the best. So far Beth's only read the newer versions."

"I've never read Nancy Drew mysteries," Christina said as they hurried up the path leading to Children's House. A fat raindrop rolled down her forehead.

Glancing skyward, Christina saw charcoal gray clouds gathering overhead. In the distance, ominous thunder rumbled.

"You've never read a Nancy Drew? Are you kidding me?" Katie cried, also checking the sky. "Everyone reads Nancy Drew. It's practically abnormal not to. Take one," she said, nodding down at the books in her arms. "Nobody in the books has mystical experiences or anything, but you might like them anyway."

Christina took a book off the top and examined the old-fashioned cover. A blond girl, Nancy Drew, dressed in a long narrow skirt and pink sweater set, held a flashlight and climbed an eerie staircase. "I wonder if Nancy Drew had a guardian angel," Christina mused aloud, reminded of how Ned, Norma, and Edwina seemed to move effortlessly through time.

Katie laughed. "She must have had one. She's always getting out of the worst messes. A guardian angel would sure explain why the things she needs always seem to turn up, things like a key or a flashlight."

Two raindrops plopped onto the book cover. Christina quickly wiped them away with her purple sweatshirt and quickened her pace. "Hurry up. We're going to get soaked," she said.

A bolt of lightning shot across the sky, etching a jagged yellow line across the ever-darkening clouds. A startling clap of thunder banged right behind it. As if the lightning had poked a hole in the cloud, a torrent of warm rain suddenly poured down upon them.

Their heads down, the girls raced along the path, clattering up the wooden steps to the porch. Once safely protected by the porch roof, they laughed and shook water from themselves. "Poor Nancy got a little wet," Katie said, looking down at her damp books.

"This one's okay," Christina said as she took the book out from under her sweatshirt.

When they entered the building, the receptionist remembered them and nodded them through. Ms. Baker waved at them from her office as they passed by on the second floor.

In Beth and Marta's room, they found the girls standing by the window. Beth frowned, her arm draped consolingly over Marta's shoulder. Marta wrung her hands, danced around nervously, and seemed near tears.

"What's wrong?" Christina asked, rushing to them.

Marta's eyes were wide and anguished. She opened her mouth to speak, but only little croaking sounds came out.

"It's her kitten," Beth explained. "He's stuck outside in the rain."

Christina peered out the window, trying to locate Raindrop. It was hard to see through the rain, which blanketed the glass in translucent sheets. In a short time, the storm had picked up tremendous force. The newly budding trees seemed to dance wildly, their branches lashed by a ferocious wind.

The sloped roof outside the window glistened in the rain. Water ran off its tiles in wide streams. Across the way, another section of the house jutted out, water overflowing its wooden drain gutters. "I don't see him," Christina said, searching the rooftops.

"Oh, no! He fell!" Marta shouted, frantically pressing her face and small hands against the window in order to see for herself. "No! No! He's still there. I see him. He's on that gutter across the way, on the other roof. Oh, I know he's going to fall off. Oh, no!"

"How did he get out there?" Katie asked.

"Marta was standing by the window with him. She was watching you and Christina come up the path," Beth explained. "We heard Nurse Worly out in the hall. She was about to come in."

"It wasn't raining then. Not hard. So I opened the window and put him outside to hide him," Marta said in a tear-choked voice. "By the time she left the room, it had started pouring." Marta crunched her face down hard as she fought back tears. Her temples and cheeks reddened with her effort at self-control, and Christina thought she'd never seen a more pitiful sight.

She looked out the rain-soaked window again and this time spotted the kitten. He stood whimpering on the drain where the two sections of the house joined. "I'll get him for you," Christina said.

"Are you crazy?" Katie cried.

"I'll be careful," Christina said, pushing up the window. "He's just a few feet away. He's not even close to the edge of the roof. Don't worry."

"Be careful," Katie said anxiously as Christina perched on the windowsill. "Hey, wait. I know. Wait." She yanked the crisp, white topsheet off Beth's bed. "Hold onto this," she said, handing a corner of the sheet to Christina. "I'll tie the other end to this radiator rung here by the window."

"All right," Christina agreed, taking hold of one end of the sheet. "Don't worry, Marta. I'll have him for you in a second."

Stepping out onto the roof, Christina ducked her head away from the pelting rain. The wind tossed her hair across her face, and small rivers ran down the collar of her sweatshirt.

Raindrop mewed plaintively, clinging to the drain as if it were the only thing keeping him from being washed away.

With one hand against the outside wall of the house and the other clutching the sheet, Christina took tiny steps out onto the roof. Moving slowly, with deliberate actions, she closed in on the crying kitten. In minutes, she was near him.

Fearing that he might run, Christina moved cautiously. "Hi, Raindrop," she cooed. "Got a little wet, didn't you, kitty? Everything's okay now. Come to me." She reached out with her one free hand and scooped up the whimpering ball of dripping black fur. Cradling him in the crook of her arm, she began her return trip in tiny, careful steps.

Poor little thing, she thought as she neared the window. He was lucky to have Marta to look after him. He meant so much to Marta, too. Strange how a small creature like Raindrop could make such a huge difference in the life of a little girl. Christina felt happy she'd been able to get him back for Marta.

At the window, Katie reached out and Christina handed her the wet kitten. "Way to go!" Katie cheered, handing Raindrop to Marta, whose face lit with happiness.

With her back still pressed against the outside wall, Christina tossed her end of the sheet into the window and breathed a sigh of relief. She'd made it. Marta would be happy again. Christina reached up to steady herself on the rooftop above her as she turned, preparing to re-enter the window.

She stepped, and the tile beneath her shot out from under her foot.

"No!" Katie screamed as Christina flew over backward.

"Oh!" Christina cried out in shock and terror as she hit the tile roof on her back. Then she realized she was sliding, sliding fast down the wet roof.

She clawed at the tiles, desperate for something to hold on to. But there was nothing.

8

Christina was having the dark dream again. The one where she struggled through complete, absolute darkness. Not a glimmer of light made it through the blackness.

Don't worry, she told herself. *You know it's only a dream. You've had this dream before. Don't be scared.*

It was the same as the last time. She couldn't see a thing, but she felt she had to get somewhere. Find something. Her mother? An angel.

Slowly, noise filtered through to her, low, distant sounds. A wheel creaked somewhere as something rolled along a floor. A door opened with a squeak. In the distance, someone was speaking gently.

Christina strained her eyes, pulling to see something. Anything. Where was the doorway that opened to the room holding the luminous angel? When would she reach it? Soon, she hoped. This oppressive darkness was unnerving. But she could put up with it because she knew the gorgeous angel would soon appear. And because it was only a dream.

The voices around her grew louder, as if someone were approaching. She knew one of the voices.

It was her mother's voice.

Wait. Her mother's voice wasn't supposed to be in this dream.

"Oh, where is she? Where is she?" her mother cried, sounding nearly hysterical.

"She's right in here, Ms. Kramer," a man said. "She's sleeping right now."

Am I sleeping? Christina wondered. *Yes, I'm dreaming. I must be sleeping.* Christina moved her fingers and felt a starched cloth. She became aware of a familiar smell.

It was a hospital smell. The same as in Children's House.

A searing pain shot through her left side. She hadn't noticed it before, but it was there now, strong, biting into her like a creature with terrible gnashing teeth.

Wake up! she commanded herself, and then realized she was awake.

But everything was still black. And the pain was still tearing into her.

"Oh, Christina. My Christina." She heard her mother's emotion-loaded voice. "You're awake. How do you feel?"

Christina forced her eyes wide. She still couldn't see. Panicked, she tried to get up, but the pain threw her back. Struggling, feeling like an animal ensnared in some hideous trap, she fought her way back up to sitting. "Mom!" she shouted, frantic with terror. "Mom! Where are you!"

"I'm here, Christina. Don't you see me?"

9

Time passed, but it was strange time. Christina slept a great deal. The medicine they gave her to kill the pain made her very sleepy. It clouded her mind. She heard people coming and going—doctors, nurses, her mother—but their voices were garbled and she couldn't really concentrate on what they were saying. She heard the words but the words made no sense, as though they were only sounds unconnected to any meaning. Because she was unable to see people, their presence was a floating, unreal thing.

After a while, Christina's medicine was reduced and her head began to clear. She became aware that her arm was in a cast and bandages were on her face. Her mother told her she'd broken her arm and cracked her cheekbone.

Christina grew anxious to leave the hospital. It seemed they poked her constantly, taking her temperature, drawing blood, testing her blood pressure. Without the changing light to guide her through the days and nights, her existence seemed free-floating. Medical procedures punctuated the time in between sleeping and listening to the boring drone of the TV set in her room.

Ashley, Molly, and Katie came to visit. "I'm so sorry," Katie said in a low voice. "I should never have let you go out there. I blame myself. You don't know how terrible I feel."

"Not as terrible as I do." Christina forced a dark stab at humor.

"No, I suppose not," Katie said gloomily.

"I was kidding," Christina said. "It wasn't your fault. You told me not to go."

Ashley sat on the bed and rubbed Christina's back. "Funny, I can tell it's you, Ashley," Christina said. "I never realized you smell like hay and lavender soap."

"Can you see anything at all?" Molly asked.

"No. But after my eye operation, I'll be okay."

Finally, one day, she felt her mother's warm hand on her cheek. "The doctor says you can come home today, honey," she said.

"No," Christina said. "That's not right. I'm not better yet." As much as she wanted to leave, she'd assumed she would go home when she was better. She would leave the hospital seeing, not still cloaked in the awful darkness.

Alice sighed. "It's going to take time, Christina. You don't need to stay here anymore. You can continue healing at home."

"But what about my operation? You told me they were going to fix my eyes." The timbre of her voice climbed as panic took hold. She clutched her mother's arm. This talk of an eye operation had been the thing she'd clung to. She wouldn't be blind forever. There was something that could be done about it. That's what her mother had said. What had changed?

"We're going to have to consult a specialist about that," her mother told her. "I've already contacted a Dr. Hernandez in the city. He's supposed to be one of the best. We have an appointment for next week."

"All right," Christina said, relieved. "All right, I guess."

* * *

Dear Dream Journal—It's the strangest thing. I can see now only when I'm asleep. In my dreams, everything is bright and clear as it ever was. Only, of course, things are strange and a bit disconnected, as dreams sometimes are. So it seems that at night I travel to this strange world that is more real than the black hole I live in during the day. But the world is so odd it makes me feel like Alice in Wonderland. It looks like my horoscope was right after all. My life has certainly changed.

* * *

"Does anyone see my sweater?" Christina asked Katie, Molly, and Ashley one day when they came to take her out.

"It's here, on the couch," Ashley said. "It is sort of cool out, especially for July. I'll help you put it on." She draped the light crocheted purple sweater over Christina's shoulders.

Christina slipped her right arm into the sleeve and pulled the left side over her cast. Gingerly, she touched her still-tender cheekbone. The bandages were off, but it still hurt. "How does my face look?" she asked.

"Fine," Molly said quickly.

"Your face is fine, but there's still a pretty nasty-looking purple bruise on your cheek," Katie said. "It kind of travels up under your eye, too, like you have a black eye."

"It sounds lovely," Christina said dismally.

"It's not going to be there forever," Ashley said, taking hold of her right arm. "It'll go away."

"There's a big spool of kite string by the door," Christina said. "Could someone get it for me, please?"

"There's not enough wind for kite flying," Katie said.

"It's not for kite flying," Christina told her as she took the spool of string from Katie, fumbling it slightly.

"Then what's it for?" Molly asked.

"I'll show you," Christina said. "I had an idea last night."

With Ashley guiding Christina, the girls headed out of the house. "You're forgetting your bag," Katie told Molly.

"No, I'm not," Molly replied. "I'm leaving it behind so I don't have to answer the phone."

Outside, the slightly cool air felt wonderful to Christina. The breeze carried the musky smell of horses and hay to her. "What's the sky like?" she asked.

"Crystal blue," Molly told her.

"When do you leave for space camp?" Christina asked her.

"Not until the end of the month. You'll see me before I go."

"I hope so," Christina said. "Tomorrow we're going

into the city to see . . . well, to meet with . . . Dr. Hernandez."

"Great," Ashley said brightly. "I just know everything is going to be okay. Now, what do you want to do with that kite string?"

"Go to the bridge," Christina said without having to think about it.

"Are you sure you can manage it?" Molly asked.

"I'm pretty sure," Christina replied. "I feel good today, better than I've felt since the accident. I really want to see Norma, Edwina, and Ned."

"Maybe they can help you," Ashley said.

"I hope so," Christina said. "If I ever needed an angel's help, it's now."

They went behind the stable and Christina stopped them. "Take me to the corner of the stable," she requested of Ashley. As soon as she touched the stable wall, she turned. "Now walk me slowly to the nearest tree I'd reach by walking straight ahead."

Ashley guided her and Christina counted off the paces. "One, two, three . . ." In twenty paces they reached a pine. "Could you tie this string around the tree for me?" she requested.

"What are you doing?" Katie asked.

"I'm making a path I can follow to the bridge," Christina explained. "That way I can get there whenever I need to."

"That's too dangerous. I'll bring you whenever you want to go," Ashley said sternly.

"What if you're not around?" Christina said.

"You can wait for me."

"I don't want to have to depend on you. I just think now is a time when I don't want to be cut off from the bridge. Knowing it's there gives me hope, and I need to be able to reach it."

"But you can't go there yourself," Molly said.

"Please, just help me connect the string and I won't go myself," Christina said. "I just want to feel that I could, that I'm not cut off from it. Please."

"You won't go by yourself?" Ashley pressed.

"No, I won't. I'd be too scared."

"All right," Ashley agreed. "If it will make you feel better, we can connect the string."

They made their way through the woods, pulling the spool of thread from tree to tree, wrapping it around and securing it in place with knots. "It's like we're spiders making a humongous web," Katie said.

Christina marveled at how alive the smells and sounds of the woods seemed to her. She used to experience the overpowering scent of pine so strongly that any other smell in the woods was covered over by its intensity. Now, although keenly aware of the pine, she was also conscious of other smells. The sharp, damp smell of moss. The dank smell of fallen trees. As they neared the stream, she breathed in the smell and wetness of its moving current.

The silence of the woods now throbbed in her ears as though silence were a sound in itself. Then a twig would snap and a rustling of wings would whoosh by overhead. A chipmunk would chatter, a bird call. A flurry of little sounds, and then the big, engulfing silence of the woods closed in once more.

As Ashley guided her up a hill, stopping now and then to secure another length of string, Christina realized they were nearing the Angels Crossing Bridge. Hope rose up inside her like a song. She'd told herself not to expect miracles—not to hold any expectations at all—but now she faced the truth.

She couldn't help it. Her hopeful heart had beaten out the caution in her mind. It was in charge now.

A miracle was *exactly* what she'd come hoping for.

Her heartbeat quickened as they crested the hill and began going down. Why not expect a miracle? These were angels, after all. Angels! Who better to request a miracle of? "Is there anyone on the bridge?" she asked anxiously. "Do you see them?"

"I don't see anyone yet," Ashley replied, giving Christina's arm a supportive squeeze. "We're too far away to really tell, though."

They stopped several more times to tie string. "This is the last tree before the bridge, and you're out of string," Katie told Christina. "This will have to be close enough."

"Let me see if I could find it from here," Christina said, wriggling away from Ashley.

"Careful," Ashley warned as Christina stretched both hands out in front and walked blindly in what she guessed was the direction of the bridge.

Letting the rushing water of the creek guide her, she kept moving forward. A low boulder in her path tripped her up, but she recovered her balance without falling down. Soon she grabbed hold of the dry old wood of the bridge's entrance. "Made it!" she cried, feeling proud.

Groping her way along the entrance to the bridge's

wooden railing, she made her way onto the bridge. "Hello?" she whispered. "Are you there?"

Voices spoke to her. They were faint and faraway, but she was sure she heard them.

"Are you all right?" Ashley asked coming alongside her.

"Shh!" Christina said. "I heard something. Don't you hear voices?"

They listened together a moment. Christina heard it again, laughing, merrily calling voices, almost like singing. "There they are!"

"Sorry. I don't hear anything," Ashley said regretfully.

"Me neither," Katie said.

"But I hear something," Christina insisted, cocking her head and straining to identify the exact words of the babbling song. Again, she heard the lovely singsong but couldn't make it out.

"I think you must be hearing the water," Molly suggested. "I closed my eyes just now and the water sounds like someone calling to you. It echoes in the bridge."

"No," Christina insisted. "It couldn't be."

Yet, listening again, she realized Molly was right. Her soaring spirit plummeted, and she gripped the railing hard to steady herself as disappointment swept over her.

The singing, magical voice belonged only to the rushing water in the creek below.

10

Just to see if she could, Christina followed the kite string back from the bridge. It wasn't as easy as she'd imagined. It took a lot of concentration, and the string sagged in spots. Ashley, Katie, and Molly tightened it in places where it drooped to the ground.

By the time Ashley led her to her front door, she was bone tired. The effort of making her way back had wearied her, but her disappointment was what really exhausted her.

Christina felt tired in her spirit. Her inner struggle had worn her out. Inside, she fought against disappointment. She was determined not to give in to it. So what if Edwina, Norma, and Ned weren't on the bridge this time? They were out doing something wonderful in some other place, maybe in some other time.

That evening, just after supper, there was a knock at the door. "Christina, you have a visitor," her mother said.

"Hi, Christina, it's me, Matt Larson." The boy's familiar but unexpected voice floated to her from the doorway. He sounded awkward, nervous.

Surprised and flustered, Christina stood up from her easychair next to the rustic stone fireplace. Off balance, she stumbled back into it.

"Are you all right?" Matt asked, rushing to her side.

Christina felt her cheeks burn with an embarrassed blush. Completely mortified, she wished she could disappear. "I'm fine, really," she said with an embarrassed laugh. "I'm still not used to being unable to see."

"Have a seat," Alice offered Matt. "Would you like some lemonade?"

"Yes, please. Thanks. I mean, if it's not any trouble," he said.

"No trouble," Alice said.

Gauging the distance of his voice, Christina could tell Matt was sitting on the brown couch that faced the fireplace. "I wanted to come to the hospital, but I didn't know if I should," he said. "Molly told me you were in pretty bad shape."

"I was kind of out of it for most of the time," Christina said. As she spoke, she tried to recall the lines of his face but found she couldn't. She paid attention to his voice for the first time, though. Despite his nervousness, it was still smooth and full, warm.

"Oh, I . . . uh . . . I brought this letter for you," he said. She heard a crumpling paper sound as he took the letter from his jeans pocket. "I suppose I should read it to you, huh?" he said awkwardly. "It's from Marta."

Christina smiled. She hadn't even thought about Marta since her accident. "Marta," she said fondly. "How is she?"

"I don't think she's great," Matt said seriously. "She has leukemia. They just found out yesterday, when the results of her tests came back. Dr. Sebruch told me."

Leukemia! Christina pressed her back into the chair as if the news had hit her like a baseball. Leukemia! She'd had no idea Marta was that sick! This was terrible; that poor little girl. "I know leukemia is very serious, but what is it, exactly?"

"Leukemia is cancer of the blood," Alice said, her voice coming from next to Matt. "The body produces too many white blood cells."

"But aren't white blood cells good? Don't they fight infections?" Christina questioned, remembering the science lesson on blood cells she'd had toward the end of school.

"As I understand it, these white blood cells aren't very effective ones. They don't fight infection well, and they crowd out the red cells," Alice continued. "I believe that leukemia is the most common form of cancer in children."

"Is Marta going to . . . is she going to . . . die?" Christina asked.

"Dr. Sebruch told me that there's a lot they can do," Matt told her. "But Marta may need a bone marrow transplant."

"The bone marrow produces the blood cells, right?" Christina said.

"I think so," Matt replied.

"Does she need a bone marrow donor?" Christina asked. Silently, she resolved to be that donor if she was able to.

"No, Marta's mother is doing that," Matt told her. "But they're still waiting for more test results." He paused a moment.

Christina let the silence hang between them.

She was still absorbing the news of Marta's serious illness. In her mind's eye, she saw those sparkling eyes and the bright smile. How could she be so sick?

"Should I read you the letter?" Matt asked.

"Yes, please."

"Dear Christina," he began reading. "I hope you are feeling better. I am very, very, very, very, very sorry that you fell off the roof and hurt yourself. It was all my fault, and I feel so, so, so, so, so bad. Thank you for saving Raindrop. He is fine. I think he has a little cold, though. He keeps sneezing. Yesterday he sneezed when Nurse Worly was in the room. He was hiding under my blanket. I covered my nose so she would think it was me who sneezed. She said, 'Bless you,' to me. Wouldn't it have been funny if Raindrop said thank you in a little cat voice? I hope you feel better real, real, real soon. I can't wait until you come and visit me again. Love and kisses, your very, very, very good friend, Marta."

"She's so sweet," Christina said. "She sounds happy."

"She doesn't know about the leukemia yet," Matt said. "I wonder if she'll really even understand when they tell her."

"Does she know I'm blind?" Christina asked.

"I don't think so," Matt replied. "She only knows you fell and broke your arm."

"That's good," Christina said. "I wouldn't want her to be upset."

"Are you going to go see her?" Matt asked.

"After my operation," Christina told him. "When I'm better, I'll see her. That way she won't be upset."

"I see what you mean," Matt said. "I'll just tell her you're still not feeling very well."

"That would be good."

"Would you like more lemonade, Matt?" Alice offered.

"No, thanks, Mrs. Kramer, I should go now, anyway." With a soft whoosh of fabric, Christina heard him get off the couch. "Good luck with your operation, Christina. When is it going to be?"

"We don't know," Alice told him. "We're going to see the specialist tomorrow."

"Well, good luck, anyway," Matt said, his voice moving toward the front door.

"Thanks for coming," Christina said. "Thanks a lot."

"No problem. Bye."

"What a nice boy," Alice said after he'd gone.

"Yeah," Christina agreed. "Real nice. He's Molly's boyfriend."

"Oh," Alice said, sounding a little disappointed by the news. "Oh, well, it was nice of him to come see you."

Come see you. The phrase repeated in Christina's head. Would she ever be able to go *see* anyone again?

She had to believe she would. She had to believe Dr. Hernandez could help her.

Just before bed, the phone rang. "It's me," Molly said when Christina answered the phone. "My dad wants you to use his apartment where he stays when he stays in the city," she said. "You know, for when you go to see the doctor tomorrow."

"Wow, that's nice of him," Christina said. "Matt came by." She felt like she had to tell Molly this, so she wouldn't think anything sneaky was going on.

"He's been worried about you," Molly said, not sounding put out. "He likes you a lot."

Christina smiled at this. But then she worried about how Molly felt about it. "Is . . . Is . . . that all right with you?"

"Oh, sure," Molly said. "He likes you as a friend. You know. I'm not the jealous type, anyway. My dad wants to talk to your mom. I'll talk to you tomorrow."

"Okay. Bye." Christina called her mother and handed her the phone. "Mr. Morgan wants to talk to you."

Christina heard a sigh of relief in her mother's voice as she spoke to Molly's father. Using the apartment instead of going to a hotel would save a lot of money.

As she listened to them talk, she wondered about Molly. She was glad her friend hadn't been upset about Matt coming over. But she wondered why she wasn't. Was it because she just wasn't the jealous type, as she said? Was it because she didn't care that much about Matt? Or was it because she didn't think Matt could ever be interested in Christina as a girlfriend?

Stop even thinking about it, she scolded herself. Matt was Molly's boyfriend, and that was that.

Christina went to bed early, falling asleep quickly, but it wasn't a restful sleep. She tossed in her bed, knotting the sheets around her long legs. Finally, her eyes snapped open.

It took her a moment to realize where she was. Nothing she could think of was more disturbing, more disorienting, than opening her eyes only to find herself still engulfed in blackness.

But, slowly, the sounds of the night filtered through her half-open window. The steady, clicking song of crickets. The pulsing undertone of croaking toads. Summer night sounds.

Christina fumbled under her pillow until she found her dream journal and felt-tipped pen. She still remembered how to make the letters even though she couldn't visually check their shape.

> Dear Dream Journal—I dreamed of a bat again tonight. But this time, the bat was leading me somewhere. It was shadowy, but I think I was in the woods. I was frightened, very frightened. Somehow I knew I should follow the bat, though. It led me to a plain tin box, which I couldn't open. I banged on the box and threw it against a tree, desperate to open it. Then the bat landed on the ground and turned into a big black key. Something told me that the key would open the box, but I was afraid to pick up the black bat key.

Christina stopped writing. What did the bat and the key mean? What was in the box? Did the bat mean her harm or was it trying to help? She hated the idea that she might never find out.

Part of her wanted to hurry back to sleep in the hope of continuing the dream. If the dream came again, she would pick up the key, she told herself.

Another part of Christina hoped the dream was gone for good. Maybe it meant nothing. Perhaps dreams were only silly, strange stories the mind concocted while the rest of the body slept.

No. She believed dreams were important. What did this one mean?

With the dream journal still open on her lap, Christina drifted back to sleep. She dreamed again, but this time she was in sunlight, in a field. Rays of sun warmed her cheeks.

And then, suddenly, she was outside herself, looking at herself. She was dancing in the field, dancing in a loose yellow, flowered cotton dress. Barefoot. Happy. And rainbow-colored light floated in ribbons of color from out of her eyes.

11

Dr. Hernandez had a deep, warm voice with a soft Spanish accent. He spoke slowly, seeming to pick his words carefully. "Here's the thing," he said to Christina and Alice, sitting in front of his desk. "We can't be certain until we try, but I think our chances for success using laser surgery are good."

Christina's heart leaped at his words. They were exactly what she'd hoped to hear.

"My examination just now was really superficial," he went on. "This afternoon you will go to Angel of Mercy Hospital for more tests. I'll get the results by tomorrow morning, and then I'll know for certain if you will be a good candidate for the type of laser surgery I am thinking of."

"How will you know?" Alice asked. "What will you be looking for?"

"A blood clot. Because Christina incurred her blindness through a fall, I suspect there may be a small blood clot blocking one of the veins to her eyes. In this type of retinopathy, the clot sometimes dissolves on its own, but since it hasn't done so thus far, I think we will have to use laser surgery."

"Retinopathy?" Christina questioned.

"Yes. It refers to your retina, the layer of light-sensitive cells in the back of your eyeball. In cases like this, there is a danger that the retina will deteriorate from the lack of blood reaching it. We will want to schedule this operation very quickly in order to keep that retinal deterioration from happening."

"What if it does happen?" Alice asked.

"Once the retina is damaged, the effects are most often irreversible."

Irreversible. Not reversible. No going back. Christina's brain went over this information until it exploded within her like a flaming fireball. "You mean I could be blind forever?" Christina cried. Alice laid her hand over Christina's, gripping it.

"It's possible, but let's be hopeful," Dr. Hernandez said. "I am."

Christina was suddenly nauseated. Her stomach lurched. "Mom, I need a bathroom," she said urgently. "I'm sick."

"Excuse us," her mother said as she hurried Christina out of the office and down the hall. By the time they reached a bathroom, though, Christina's stomach had settled.

"Mom! I can't be blind forever!" Christina cried, clinging to her mother's arm. "I can't!"

"You won't, honey. Think positive. He said your chances are good."

"But what if my retina, or whatever it is, is already too damaged? What if it's irreversible?"

Alice pulled Christina to her and hugged her firmly. "It's not going to be too damaged. It's going to be fine. It will be."

As much as Christina longed to take comfort in her mother's hopeful words, she couldn't. Alice was only saying what she hoped would be true. She had no proof. And Christina could feel the fear lurking behind her mother's bravery. She was only talking to make them both brave. But talking was just words.

That afternoon, at Angel of Mercy Hospital, Christina clung to the warmth of her mother's hand, lost in a sea of strange voices, smells, and sounds as she went through a series of tests. "At least this place has a good name," she said to her mother as a nurse placed something that felt like a plastic helmet on her head.

"That's right. You and your angels," said Alice lightly. Oddly enough, with all her mystical beliefs, Alice just couldn't accept the idea of angels.

"All right now, lie still," the nurse said, lowering Christina onto a table. "We're going to get some pictures of the inside of your head."

The tests weren't painful. At the most, they were a little uncomfortable at times. But by the time they reached Mr. Morgan's apartment, Christina was emotionally exhausted as well as physically tired.

"What a gorgeous place," Alice commented as she led Christina into the apartment. "It was so nice of the Morgans to let us use it. It must be nice to be wealthy."

"I never thought you cared about money that much,"

Christina said, settling into a wonderfully soft velvet chair.

"Money isn't really all that important to me," Alice said. "But when you don't have enough, it just seems like life would be simpler if you were wealthy."

"This is costing a lot of money, isn't it?" Christina asked, thinking about the cost of her accident for the first time.

Her mother smoothed the top of her hair. "Don't worry about money, sweetie. I've got enough."

They ordered Chinese food delivered to the door, and then spent the evening in front of the TV. Her mother explained anything Christina couldn't understand from the sound.

At around nine o'clock, the phone rang.

"Hello, Doctor," Alice said.

Christina froze where she was sitting. What had he found? Why was he calling so late? Was it bad news? It had to be. Why else would he be calling?

"Yes. All right. I understand. Thank you for calling. Bye," Alice said.

"What, Mom? What?" Christina asked, her voice quivering. "You can tell me."

Alice came next to Christina's chair and knelt close. "It's a clot, and Dr. Hernandez wants to operate early tomorrow morning."

"So . . . it's . . . it's good news, really," Christina said. "Isn't it?"

"Yes," Alice said. "It is good news. Now, let's get you to bed. You should be well-rested for tomorrow."

"Okay. I'm awfully tired, anyway."

As she lay in the strange bed that night, listening to the unfamiliar city sounds, Christina realized how frightened she was about tomorrow. She'd never had an operation before. The only time she'd been in a hospital before the accident was when she'd fallen off a horse many years ago and had to get stitches. Tomorrow would be much more serious than that. The thought of it terrified her.

To calm herself, Christina tried to envision Ned, Norma, and Edwina sitting on the bridge. The picture came to her easily. She saw their good, happy faces and felt better right away. "Help me tomorrow, please," she murmured out loud. "Please be with me," she said, and then she drifted off into a dreamless sleep.

12

The last thing Christina remembered was the anesthesia. She breathed in through a mask, and the sweet-smelling medicine pulled her down into unconsciousness.

Hours later she slowly awakened. Her aching, sore eyes felt too heavy to open. She struggled to do it, but then gave up. Her eyes were covered with bandages, anyway. It wouldn't have been any use. She wouldn't have known if she could see or not.

She fell back to sleep and dreamed of the tin box. She turned the black bat key in the lock and it sprang open. Inside was a piece of folded paper. She reached in, took the paper, and unfolded it. A capital *I* was the only thing written on the paper.

I? Christina wondered about it as she came out of the dream and floated up to consciousness. *I*. Eye. Of course. The dream had to do with her eyes.

Waking up, she became aware that something was happening around her.

"Good, she's coming around," Dr. Hernandez said.

"How do you feel, sweetie?" her mother asked, taking her hand.

"All right, I think," Christina replied in a raspy voice.

"The anesthesia makes your throat dry," Dr. Hernandez said as he continued working on her bandages. It sounded like he was snipping them off. "I just want to find out what you can see, Christina, then we'll replace the bandages at least until tomorrow," he said.

"Will she be able to see when the bandages come off?" Alice asked anxiously.

"Possibly. Hopefully," Dr. Hernandez replied.

To see again! To see her mother's face, her friends— anything and everything in the entire world. How she'd taken her sight for granted before! Never again. From now on she intended to drink in all the colors, all the beauty around her.

"All right, how is it?" Dr. Hernandez asked.

"What do you mean?" Christina asked.

"You don't see anything?" he questioned.

Christina's hands flew to her face. Her bandages were off!

"It's all still black," she cried. "I can't see anything! Oh, Mom! I can't see at all!"

Alice held Christina tightly. "Are you sure? The doctor is shining a light in your eyes. Can you see any light at all?" Her voice was urgent with tightly reined panic.

Tears flooded Christina and she let them pour down her cheeks.

"Nothing at all?" Dr. Hernandez questioned softly. "A spot of grayish light, perhaps? Or floating specks of colored light?"

"Nothing!" Christina sobbed. "Nothing at all!"

13

Christina stared out the window, peering hard into the darkness that engulfed her. She knew she was staring out an open window because a warm breeze swept strands of hair around her face, and she heard the familiar summer sounds of the ranch—birds calling to one another, the whinny and sputter of horses, cars and pickup trucks pulling up and down the dirt road in front of her cabin.

"Are you going to just stand by that window all day?" Ashley's voice seemed to float to her.

Christina turned quickly toward the sound. As she did, she put on the dark sunglasses in her hand. "I didn't even hear you come in," she said.

Ashley's voice grew closer. "I guess not. Cool shades."

Christina felt self-conscious about the sunglasses and laughed anxiously. "I don't want to weird people out with the way my eyes look."

"You look all right," Ashley said. "Your eyes look normal."

Christina took her glasses off. "Are you sure?"

"Uh-huh, your eyes look the same. I think maybe you're blinking a little less often than normal, but otherwise, no problem."

Christina put the dark glasses back on. "If I'm blinking less, then I want to wear them. I don't want to look strange, like I'm staring at people or something."

"You don't," Ashley assured her. "When I came in you were looking out the window so hard I would have thought you were seeing something. What were you doing? Listening to something?"

"I was," Christina said. "I hear the sounds around here so much more than before. I was noticing the smells, too. Lately the smells around me seem very loud."

"Loud?" Ashley questioned.

Christina nodded. "I don't know how else to say it. I'm so much more aware of them. I can smell the horses and the hay, and the dryness in the air today. I can smell the colognes people wear, even the soaps they use. You just used some kind of herbal shampoo, didn't you?"

Ashley laughed. "This morning I washed my hair with Herb Green shampoo. That's pretty good."

Christina let out a bitter chuckle. "Yeah, it's great."

Ashley put her hand on Christina's arm. "I know you'd rather have your eyesight back," she said sympathetically.

There was a moment of uncomfortable silence between them. Christina didn't want to be bitter and self-pitying, but she couldn't help it. She'd been so sure the operation would work. Dr. Hernandez had seemed shocked that it hadn't. "It might work yet," he told Christina and her mother on the day Christina left the hospital. "Your eyes might simply need some time to readjust." But he also said there might have been more damage to the retina than he'd thought. He scheduled an appointment for them to return in two weeks. He would run more tests then.

"Do you know what smell really drives me crazy?" Christina asked at last. "The smell of pine from the woods."

"You can smell that all the way from here?" Ashley asked, surprised.

"Yes. I never noticed it before, but now I smell it day and night. And it's as if the smell is there just to make me think about the woods, just to remind me that the angels aren't going to help me."

"Oh, Christina," Ashley said in a sorrowful voice. "They might still come through. You know they work in odd ways."

"How long am I supposed to wait?" Christina lashed out at her. The forceful fury behind her own words startled her. She hadn't realized she felt so angry. Angry and hurt. Where were the angels? Why had they abandoned her, forgotten her?

For that matter, why had they deserted little Marta and all those children in the hospital? What good were angels if they only helped whomever and whenever they pleased?

"You can't give up on the angels," Ashley said softly.

"Why can't I?" Christina snapped. "They've given up on me."

"You don't know that," Ashley argued.

"Sure I do," Christina said. "I'm facing you, Ashley, and

I might know what shampoo you used. I even know you've been riding from the horsey smell on you. But I don't know what you're wearing, or how your hair is fixed. I can't see you smile, or see what's happening outside this window. I want to see, Ashley! I want my eyes back." Christina stopped and unclenched her hands, which she'd balled into angry fists as she spoke. She breathed deeply, as she always did to calm herself. When she spoke again, her words were biting and resentful. "The angels don't care. They're off busy with something more important, like car thieves or other wonderful people like that, people who *really* need them, not unimportant little blind girls like me."

"Christina, I've never heard you talk like this," Ashley said. "You don't even sound like yourself."

As she spoke, a knock sounded at the door. "I'll get it," Ashley offered.

"Tell whoever it is to go away," Christina muttered. She was in no mood for company. She heard Ashley open the door. The female voice on the other side was unusual, yet familiar.

"Hello, Christina," the voice said, warmly and kindly, with a soft East Indian accent.

"Dr. Sebruch," Christina said, surprised that the doctor had come to see her. She wanted to ask her directly why she'd come but thought it would be rude. "Would you like to sit down?"

"Thank you." She took Christina's arm and guided her over to the couch. After asking how Christina was feeling and about her operation, Dr. Sebruch got to the point. "Marta would love a visit from you."

"How is Marta?" Christina asked.

"Low," Dr. Sebruch said in a matter-of-fact way. "She now understands how serious her condition is. She's frightened and feels very lonely. Her mother comes, of course, but her mother is frightened, too, and Marta senses it."

"I'm not exactly in the greatest spirits myself these days," Christina replied. "Don't you think it might upset her even more to see me the way I am?"

"No," Dr. Sebruch said.

"Well, I think it would," Christina replied, not meaning her words to sound as surly as they came out. "I'm sorry, Dr. Sebruch, but I can't go. How can I help her when I can't even help myself?"

"I can see that you are feeling badly," Dr. Sebruch said. "And you have every right to, I'm sure. Yet, helping others can sometimes be a strong tonic for an ailing spirit."

Unintentionally, a scornful cough caught in Christina's throat. "It's not my *spirit* that's the problem. It's my eyes."

"Spirit and health are very intertwined," Dr. Sebruch countered gently. From the rustle of fabric, Christina could tell the doctor had gotten to her feet. "Please consider coming to see Marta."

"I can't *see* anybody," Christina said.

"You will be able to see Marta nonetheless," Dr. Sebruch said. To Christina's surprise, she planted a gentle kiss on the top of her head. The pleasant smell of lavender floated around Christina, and for the briefest moment, her heart felt light with hope. But the feeling quickly vanished.

"Good-bye, Dr. Sebruch," Ashley said, obviously walking the doctor to the door.

"Good-bye," Christina echoed, suddenly worried that she'd been rude to the woman.

"I hope to see you soon," Dr. Sebruch said from the door. "Good-bye, dear Christina."

"What a nice woman!" Ashley said passionately as she shut the door.

"Was I rude?" Christina fretted.

"A little bit snotty, yeah," Ashley said honestly. "But she didn't seem to mind. She has such unusual eyes."

"They're dark and sort of mysterious," Christina recalled.

"There's a little speck of gold in each eye, too," Ashley said.

"I never noticed that," Christina admitted absently. She was only half listening. Inside, she was worrying about being rude to Dr. Sebruch. She never used to be rude to people before, especially nice people like the doctor. Yet the woman had angered her in a way she didn't entirely understand.

She pounded the arm of the couch. "I didn't want to be rude to her, but she's got a lot of nerve coming here, if you think about it."

"Nerve?" Ashley asked, stunned.

"Yeah, nerve! I have a few problems of my own right now, in case she hadn't noticed. I can't exactly believe that the sight of me stumbling blindly around her room is going to make Marta feel better. I can't even read the poor kid a book!"

"You could talk to her," Ashley suggested gently.

"What am I going to say, 'Gee, Marta, don't worry. Everything will be all right. Look how swell everything has turned out for me'?"

"Oh, my gosh, Christina, I can't believe how angry you are," Ashley said. "Your attitude isn't going to help matters."

"Who are you to say?" Christina snapped at her friend. "Talk about nerve! You're kind of nervy, yourself. You can see, can't you?"

"Of course. Of course I can," Ashley said defensively. "But that doesn't mean—"

"It means you don't know what it feels like, so you should have nothing to say about the subject," Christina cut her off.

"You are in *some* mood today," Ashley said, sounding angry. "I'm going. I hope you feel better."

"Good-bye," Christina snapped.

About a half hour after Ashley had gone, Christina rose from the couch and groped her way toward her bedroom, her arms stretched in front, feeling from side to side. "Ah!" she cried out, startled as her searching hand swatted a lampshade.

The lamp clattered to her feet, and she heard the sound of shattering glass. In her surprise, she stumbled back and her sunglasses fell to the ground. "Oh, no!" she gasped, knowing she'd knocked down the lamp with the cranberry-colored glass base and the flock of cardinals on the shade—the one that had belonged to her grandmother, the one her mother treasured.

"My lamp!" Alice cried from the doorway. Her mother had picked the worst possible moment to step into the house. She rushed toward Christina, and then bent down and began pushing shards of glass together.

"Is it ruined?" Christina asked, her voice quivering.

"I'm afraid so," Alice said gloomily.

Christina started to shake all over, not because she feared her mother's anger, but because she knew how much the lamp meant to her. "I'm so sorry, Mom. I didn't mean to . . . I . . . I don't know . . . I didn't expect it to be there, and I wanted to get to my room." Her face tightened as she fought back tears. It was no use. The tears rushed forward.

"It's just a lamp, Christina," Alice said soothingly.

"But it was Grandma's," Christina sobbed.

Alice put her arm around Christina. "It's all right, honey. It really is. Grandma wouldn't want you to cry over it."

"It's not all right," Christina said, burying her face in her hands. "Nothing will ever be all right again."

14

Dear Dream Journal—Tonight I dreamed of wings. It was the weirdest dream. I was walking in the dark. I couldn't see, just like I can't see when I'm awake. But I felt the feathery, soft brush of wings against my cheeks. Then I felt the wings against my arms and my neck. The wings were fluttering and they made a breeze. The smell of lavender was carried on the breeze. And suddenly, I could see. What I saw were wings of all different pastel colors, a whole crowd of them all around me. I reached out to make my way through the wings. I couldn't believe how soft they felt, like baby's skin or flower petals. I saw that the wings belonged to beautiful shining angels who smiled at me as I passed by. I pushed through the wings and felt surrounded by love, and I became so happy that tears of happiness rolled down my cheeks. I wanted to stay in the dream forever, except that

> the sound of something very loud filled my
> dream and I woke up.

The very loud sound was thunder. Christina awakened suddenly and heard rain pounding on the rooftop. Then, bang! Another clap of thunder shook the room, as if the thunder cloud were sitting right on top of her cabin.

When she was done writing in her dream journal, Christina longed to be back in the dream, to feel again the touch of the impossibly soft angel wings, to feel the all-encompassing love, to *see*—to *see* the smiles of all those glorious, radiant angels.

Thunder exploded overhead again. "The sound of angels bowling," she said softly as she lifted her head to the sound. She remembered long ago, when her grandmother was still living, that the slight white-haired lady had explained thunder to her that way. Back then, Christina had liked that idea a lot. She still liked the happy image it conjured in her head. How easy it was to imagine Ned, Norma, and Edwina laughing and clapping as they knocked down bowling pins, which fell against one another thunderously on a bed of dark, pillowy rain cloud.

She pictured Ned, Norma, and Edwina, and slowly her fond smile faded. Her head fell forward in despair. How could they have forgotten her?

After a few gloomy minutes, though, a defiant expression reshaped the crestfallen configuration of her face. "I won't let them forget me," she said softly. "I'll make them notice me."

"If that stable roof is still leaking, I'd better make sure

Daisy and Bridey have dry hay," Alice said the next morning. "Their stalls are right under the leak."

"Do you think the rain will stop?" Christina asked from the kitchen counter, where she sat finishing her breakfast of granola and herbal tea.

There was a pause while Alice went and checked the weather outside the window. "It might clear," she said. "The clouds seem to be blowing past, and the rain is down to a drizzle."

"Good," Christina said, finishing the last of her granola cereal.

"Why? Are you and your friends planning to do something special today?"

"No. Nothing much. I wanted to get outside, that's all."

"Give it a little time," Alice said as she headed for the door. Christina heard the crinkling sound of her yellow rain poncho and the squeak of her rubber boots. "Everything is still very muddy. I don't want you to slip, especially since it's . . . you know . . . it's difficult enough for you to get around right now."

"Okay. Don't worry. I'll wait."

"Christina," Alice said with a note of hesitance and uncertainty in her voice. "I was wondering if you'd be interested in getting a dog."

Christina's face lit. She'd always wanted a dog, but her mother insisted the house was too small. *Yes, a dog would be great*, she thought. But why had her mother changed her mind all of a sudden?

Then Christina realized the reason for this change of heart and her elation evaporated. "Do you mean a Seeing Eye dog?" she asked in a flat voice.

"It might help, Christina," Alice said. "It would give you more mobility and I'd worry about you less."

"No," Christina said decidedly. "I'm going to see again. We're seeing Dr. Hernandez soon, aren't we?"

"Yes. But I just thought that in the meantime—"

"No, thank you." Christina cut her off firmly. A Seeing Eye dog would mean she'd given up hoping she'd regain her eyesight. She wasn't about to do that.

"Well, we can talk some more later," Alice said. "Right now I'd better get down to the stable. Bye, sweetie."

Alice left and Christina made her way over to the front closet. She clutched each garment until she felt the cool, smooth stiffness of her rain slicker. Struggling into it took a full five minutes. Everything was so difficult now. Without sight, even the simplest task required her complete concentration. She was growing so weary of it. But it was all about to change.

"I'll go to the bridge"—she spoke quietly to herself as she fumbled along the wall toward the front door—"and I'll wait there until they notice me. I'll force the angels to notice me. I won't leave until they do."

As Christina pushed open the front door, a warm, wet mist clung to her skin. The stable was to the left. That she knew. Moving cautiously, she went down the path to the road. It was difficult to tell where the path ended and the road began. She stood, wondering if she could estimate the amount of time she'd spent walking down the path. She strained to remember back to the days when she could see. How long had it taken to walk from the road down the path to her house? Somehow she couldn't recall.

She heard the clopping sound of a horse approaching.

She must be near the road, but how near? Was she already in the road?

"You okay, Christina?" It was Jeremy, one of Ashley's two seventeen-year-old brothers. She liked Jeremy better than Jason, his twin. He was softer and nicer, and he always made Christina laugh.

"I'm a little confused," she admitted, laughing self-consciously. "I want to get to the stable."

She heard him dismounting from his horse. "Come on, I'll take you," he said, taking her arm. "I'll walk Daisy behind us." When they got to the stable, Christina took her arm back and thanked Jeremy. "I thought you wanted to go to the stable?" he questioned.

"I did, but I want to check something behind the stable," she said, not wanting to say she was going into the woods. He might try to stop her, or tell her mother, who would surely forbid her to do it.

"Okay, be careful," he said as his voice drifted toward the stable door.

Christina reached out until she felt the stable wall and followed it around to the back corner. From there, she faced the woods—she could hear the gentle call of its rustling pines—and counted off the pacing as she'd done when her friends first tied the kite string to the trees. When she counted twenty, she reached her hands out in front of her.

"Yes!" she whispered triumphantly as her fingers found the wet string tied to the first tree she came to. What a good idea it had been to have them tie the string that day. Somehow she'd known she would need to get to the bridge on her own.

Fingering the string, she set off into the deep, dripping woods.

15

Inch by inch, Christina patiently followed the string from one tree to the next. Time was impossible to gauge. Had she been in the woods a half hour or five hours? She couldn't tell. Often, her mind drifted as she went through the tedious work of following the string.

For a while she thought about Matt Larson. Would Molly break it off with him soon? She didn't seem very interested in him. And, if she did, would Matt be interested in Christina? Would he care that she couldn't see? Well, that wasn't going to last forever. She'd be sure he knew that.

Then she thought about school and wondered how she would do her work in September if she didn't have her sight back by then. Would they want her to go to a different school, one for blind kids? She didn't think there was one nearby. Would they have to move? No, she couldn't think about that. She'd have to struggle along until her next operation, or until the angels somehow worked a miracle. It was only July. Surely everything would be fine by September.

Her thoughts wandered to Marta. Katie could find out for her how the little girl was doing. She made a mental note to call Katie that night and ask.

A small boulder in her path made Christina stumble, throwing her out of her thoughts. With flailing arms, she struggled to stay balanced. Finally, she grabbed hold of a tree just before tumbling down to the soaked carpet of fallen pine needles below her.

Catching her breath, she groped in her darkness, trying to regain contact with the string. Where was it? She tried to judge the point at which she'd stumbled, moving in one direction, then the other. Had it disappeared? Maybe she'd pulled it down when she'd stumbled? After fifteen minutes of searching, she gave out a long, low growl of complete frustration. How awful to think that it might be lying right at her feet, but she couldn't find it.

And without the string, she was completely, utterly lost.

Panic rose within her, but she fought hard against it. *You're not lost*, she told herself sternly, like a strict guide scolding a panicky child. *You've been in this woods a hundred times. There must be something else you can use to find your way.*

Cocking her head, she listened hard to sounds around her. Endless dripping seemed to be the only sound. Then, slowly, she became aware of a second water sound. Was it the creek? Was she by the bridge already?

No. The sound was too gentle. It was the stream, the narrow winding stream that led to the hill just before the bridge!

Moving toward the sound, Christina stumbled into the

stream's cool center of moving water. The cool wetness rushed into Christina's sneakers, soaking her socks. She walked in the water, now confident that as long as her feet were wet, she was on the right path.

When she stepped out of the water onto the pine-laden ground, she knew she'd come to the spot where the river ran into the side of a hill. Almost instantly, she fell over a thick stick in her path. Her elbow and cheek slid along the ground, but she wasn't badly hurt. Groping at her feet, she found the stick and used it pull herself up. It would make a good walking stick.

With the stick as her support, Christina went up the hill. Soon, she felt the ground below her slope and knew she was heading for the bridge. As she descended, the ominous sound of thunder crashed in the distance. "Stop bowling and come help me," Christina said hopefully. "I need you now."

The sky opened before Christina made it to the bridge. Although she was sheltered by the canopy of pine branches overhead, more and more rain hit her the closer she got to the creek and the bridge. It ran down the neck of her rain slicker. She could feel that her hair was entirely drenched.

She estimated that she had to be nearing the bridge but soon became worried. Perhaps she'd misjudged and was heading down to the creek or had gone off in another direction, heading back into the woods.

"Ahh!" she cried, jumping back as something slammed to the ground right in front of her. From the sound, she guessed a tree or a branch had fallen in her path. Had lightning struck it? Thunder crashed overhead. A strong wind whipped her wet hair around her head.

Not far off, another crashing sound told her another branch had come down.

Where was the bridge? She turned in every direction, totally disoriented now. Arms outstretched, she moved forward. Where were Norma, Edwina, and Ned? Didn't they live by the bridge? Couldn't they see her?

She heard the babbling water of the creek but couldn't judge its distance. At least she was near it. The important thing was to keep moving. Eventually she had to come upon something.

The heel of Christina's sneaker suddenly slid on a patch of slick, wet moss. Her feet flew up from beneath her, and she was on her bottom, sliding, sliding uncontrollably. When she stopped several feet later, she felt as if she'd landed in a cold bathtub of rushing water.

The creek! Well, at least I've found this, she thought as she pulled herself to her feet. As she slogged through the water, the rain beat fiercely upon her since there were no sheltering trees over the creek. In several minutes, she came to a spot where the rushing water took on a peculiar hollow echo.

It had to be the echo of the water going under the bridge, she concluded.

Moving to the left, she stepped up onto land. As she reached out, her hand felt a wooden board, one of the bridge's bottom supports. She'd made it! In minutes she'd felt her way along the wood and onto the bridge.

She stood, dripping on the wooden floorboards, with her arms spread wide. "I'm here!" she shouted. "You can't ignore me now!"

16

Christina sat huddled in a corner of the covered bridge, listening to the steady drubbing of the relentless rain pelting the roof. The wild cracks of thunder broke the monotony of the steadily falling rain. Wind whistled through the trees. She could hear the branches flailing.

Although it was a warm day, the water on her skin, clothing, and hair had grown cold. She shivered and her teeth chattered. She'd been there such a long time; it seemed she'd never be warm and dry again.

The thunder subsided, but the rain did not. Its steady rhythm made Christina feel drowsy. She wondered how long she had been waiting for the angels. She rested her head on her bent knees. She had no idea.

Christina didn't even realize she'd fallen asleep. She was only aware that she could see now, although she wasn't shocked or amazed by the fact. It was as it used to be back when she took her sight for granted.

She was in Children's Hospital at the end of the second-floor hallway. Marta was at the other end of the hall, dressed in a white cotton nightgown that fell to her ankles. Her feet were bare and her chin-length brown hair was messy, as if she'd just awakened from sleeping. When she saw Christina, her face became luminously happy, and she reached out toward her. "Christina, you came!" she shouted, although her voice sounded very far away, farther than it should have considering the short distance between them.

"Yes, yes," Christina shouted to her. "I'm here. Don't worry. I'm here." She began to hurry toward the girl, but the hall somehow grew longer and longer as she walked. No matter how fast she moved, the distance between them remained the same.

"Hurry, Christina," Marta called. "I've missed you. Where have you been?"

"I'm trying," Christina shouted. "I can't seem to get there."

"Try!" Marta urged her. "Please, try."

Christina put her head down as though she were moving through a gale wind that kept pushing her back. She walked, pumping with her arms, determined. But when she again picked up her head, she was no closer to Marta than before.

"Christina, what's wrong?" Marta called, her voice rising and becoming even more childlike than usual. "Why don't you come?"

Christina's eyes snapped open, and she was again plummeted into darkness. "Marta?" she whispered. Only the pounding rain replied, and Christina knew then it had been a dream.

The rain beat down relentlessly. Normally, Christina might have started to pace impatiently on the bridge. She would have wandered back and forth, venturing off the bridge from time to time just to break things up. But now, sightless, she felt glued to the corner of the bridge where she sat huddled and listening to the steady rainfall.

She was very cold and wondered if the temperature had dropped or if she, herself, were simply cold from the wetness that soaked her clothes and seeped into her bones. Maybe it was night now. She had no way of knowing. The rain covered over any sound, like the hooting of an owl, that might tell if it was night or not.

Getting to her knees, she reached out into her darkness. "Where are you?" she called, a sob in her voice. "Why have you forgotten about me?" She sat back down and began to chant, but she couldn't keep her mind on it. Her head was awash with chaotic thoughts. Why had she dreamed of Marta? Where were the angels? What time was it? Why hadn't she told anyone she was coming? Oh, why had she come here at all?

Her stomach growled. Until she heard the sound, she hadn't realized she was hungry. But now, suddenly, she felt famished. Hoping there might be a candy bar in the pocket of her slicker, she reached her hand in. Her fingers wrapped around something hard. A rock.

Only a rock.

Was it a crystal? Maybe. She sometimes found small crystals in the woods and stuck them in her pocket. She closed her hand around the uneven stone and felt better. It had to be a crystal drawing good energy from the earth and the woods into her.

She clung to the crystal. It was like finding a tool, a helpmate to get her through this.

Strengthened by this thought, she got to her feet and staggered forward until she bumped into the bridge's side railing. Calmed by the crystal, she thought more clearly and realized the terrible spot she was in.

No one knew where she was. The rain might not let up for days. That happened sometimes. If she tried to find her way back, she might wind up wandering farther into the woods, more lost than ever. The woods went back for miles and miles. She had no food and was growing hungrier by the minute.

The angels were clearly not coming.

This last realization was the hardest. It was her faith in them that had led her to risk coming to the bridge by herself in the first place. But she now knew she couldn't count on them. She'd have to find a way out of this herself. She squeezed the crystal in her palm. The crystal would bring her the strength she needed to get through. It would help her draw in all the energy she needed to stay alert and to get home safely. In the very deepest place within her heart, Christina believed that though the world sometimes seemed full of sad, hurtful things, it also abounded in goodness. The crystal would help her use that good energy.

In the distance, Christina heard an animal. Lifting her head sharply, all her senses suddenly highly alert, she strained to hear. It had been a dog sound, low and whining. Were there wolves in the woods? Yes, she'd heard there were.

She clenched her crystal even more tightly. "Circle me

with good energy. Make a cocoon of good energy around me and keep me from harm," she said out loud. She knew the crystal couldn't do this on its own. She was really the one who had to encircle herself with good thoughts and call up her own deepest energy, as well as pull strength from the positive energy in the universe. But the crystal gave her something to focus on. It was a tool.

The animal sounded again, much closer this time.

Christina sagged with relief. The sound was barking. It was a dog. "Help!" she shouted. "I'm over here on the bridge. Help!"

"There she is! We found her!" Ashley's voice rang out clearly.

"Thank goodness," Christina murmured.

In minutes Ashley was next to her. "Are you all right?" she asked, wrapping her arms around Christina. "You're shivering."

"You nut! Why did you come out here alone?" Katie asked, her gruff tone undercut with concern.

Then Christina heard a beeping sound. "What's that?" she asked.

"It's me," Molly said. "I'm dialing the cellular phone. I want to phone your mother and tell her you're all right. She's crazy with worry. At least I can leave a message on her phone machine." The air filled with a scratchy, static sound. "The phone's not working," she grumbled.

"Angelic interference?" Ashley suggested.

"No," Christina said sadly. "There are no angels here."

"Sure there are," Ashley said.

"Then they're hiding," Christina replied.

"What's in your hand?" Katie asked.

Christina unfurled her fingers, revealing the crystal. "A crystal," she said.

"It's just a rock," Katie said bluntly. "A plain rock."

"It is?" Christina questioned. "Are you sure?"

"Yes," said Katie. "It looks like the kind of bluish gray stone you sometimes find in the creek."

17

"Okay, now, we're at the steps," Katie told Christina. Christina leaned on Katie as they took the first step onto the front porch of Children's House. "One more," Katie prompted.

"We're at the front door now," Katie said. "Ready to go in?"

"Ready," Christina agreed. She was nervous about seeing Marta. How should she act? Like everything was fine, as if she didn't mind being blind? She didn't want to upset the little girl. Marta had a problem of her own. A serious problem.

But she couldn't stop thinking of her dream. Because of it—the fact that it had been so real and upsetting—she had to come see Marta. There was no longer any choice. She couldn't leave things as they had been in the dream, not being able to reach Marta. She had to meet the dream's challenge, to successfully walk down the hall and reach the little girl who was calling out to her.

"Maybe you should take those sunglasses off," Katie suggested. "You don't really need them, and they look a little spooky when you wear them inside."

Christina hesitated. She felt self-conscious without the sunglasses, afraid that her eyes appeared too vacant or looked glazed over. But she decided to trust Katie. "If you say so," she said as she took off the sunglasses and put them in the pocket of her white cotton shorts.

Katie guided Christina up to the second floor. "Hello, Katie. You're back, Christina." Ms. Baker greeted them in the hallway.

"Yep, here I am," Christina replied, trying to sound bright and normal.

"Good! Marta's really missed you," Ms. Baker said.

Christina heard Ms. Baker's heels on the linoleum floor as she walked off. "Do you think she could tell I'm blind?" Christina asked.

"I don't know," Katie replied. "I couldn't tell."

"Maybe Marta won't guess, either," Christina said hopefully.

"I think you'd better tell her," Katie said. "She'd sense something was wrong and might get weirded out by it if she didn't know the truth."

Christina sighed. "I suppose you're right."

The moment they entered the room, Christina felt a soft, small hand grab her own. "Christina, I knew you would come back! Are you still hurt? I'm so sorry. It was all my fault. Are you better?"

"I feel all right," Christina said. "I'm sorry I didn't come sooner."

"Why won't you look at me?" Marta asked anxiously.

"Are you mad at me about Raindrop? Please don't be mad at me."

Christina placed her other hand on top of Marta's. "I'm not mad. I can't see. That's why I'm not looking at you." She adjusted her face, trying to aim it in the direction of Marta's voice. "Is that better?"

"Better," Katie confirmed, standing at her shoulder. "I'm going to see the new girl who just came in this week. Bye."

Katie's footsteps crossed the room. For a moment, there was silence. "Are you there, Marta?" Christina asked, waving her hand in the air in front of her.

"Why can't you see?" Marta asked. "Did it happen when you fell, because of me?"

"Yes, but it's not your fault."

"It is," Marta insisted darkly.

"No. Marta, let's go over to your bed and talk. You guide me there." Keeping hold of Christina's hand, Marta led the way to her bed. Christina felt along the hospital bed railing, and then pulled herself up. She patted the bed beside her, indicating that Marta should sit next to her. "Listen to me, Marta," she said when she could sense the girl's warm presence at her side. "Listen very carefully. I went out to get Raindrop because I wanted to. No one forced me. You didn't make me do it. Everything would have worked out fine, too, if it hadn't been for the loose tile on the roof. That's why I fell. We can blame the tile if we like."

Marta laughed sadly. "That's silly. A tile doesn't have a brain."

Christina smiled. "No. You're right. Sometimes bad

things happen and there's no one to blame."

"I know what you mean. It's like my sickness. It just happened," Marta said sympathetically.

Christina nodded and squeezed Marta's warm hand. "How are you feeling?"

"Not too good. I'm tired a lot and I feel warm. I have a fever. I don't want to be here anymore. I want to go home, but I'm having an operation next week. Then I can go home."

"Are you scared about the operation?" Christina asked. There was silence for a moment. Marta didn't seem to want to answer this question. "I'm not scared," she said finally, "but Raindrop is. He's so scared that his heart beats very, very fast every time he thinks about me having an operation. His stomach hurts, too, when he thinks about it. I have to tell him to be brave. I tell him all the time."

"I know how he feels," Christina said. "When I had an operation on my eyes, I was scared."

"You were?" Marta asked. "No, you weren't. You're not scared of anything."

Christina laughed at this, flattered that Marta thought her so brave. "It's all right to *feel* scared as long as you *act* brave," she said. As she spoke, Marta withdrew her hand and then placed a warm, purring ball of fluff in Christina's hands. "Hello, Raindrop," she said, petting the small cat. "I think he's gotten bigger since the last time I was here."

"Maybe," Marta said. "Raindrop, you listen to Christina and don't be scared anymore. Okay? He says okay."

"Can you tell what Raindrop is saying?" Christina asked, lightly amused.

"No, but I can tell what he's thinking. It sort of shows in his face," Marta told her.

"And he's not scared anymore?"

"No. He feels a lot better now because you're here."

"Good." Christina realized that she was feeling better than she'd felt in a long time. Handing Raindrop to Marta, she reached into the pocket of her shorts, bypassed the sunglasses, and pulled out a handful of individually wrapped peppermints. "Here," she said, "I brought you these. Don't let Nurse Worly see them."

"Thanks," said Marta, scooping up the candies. "Is the rock for me, too?"

Christina hadn't realized she'd taken the rock out of her pocket along with the candies. Despite its plainness, she'd clung to it, keeping it with her, grateful that it had helped her through her frightening time on the bridge. "It's my lucky rock," she said. "I want you to have it."

Marta plucked the rock from her palm. "Wow! Thank you. Your lucky rock. It's beautiful," she said with complete sincerity. "Are you sure you want to give it away?"

"No, I don't mind, since I'm giving it to you. Do you really think it's beautiful? I've never seen it."

"You haven't? Too bad. It's got the most beautiful blue lines running all through it, and there's a little streak of silver in the middle," Marta reported. "It's very beautiful."

"Funny," Christina said. "Katie told me it was plain."

"She must not have looked closely," Marta said. "This is the most beautiful rock I've ever seen, and I'm always going to keep it with me."

Marta handed Raindrop back to Christina. "Here, he wants to come to you again."

Christina smiled as she petted the warm, purring animal. Visiting Marta was doing her as much good as it was doing Marta, maybe even more so. "I'm glad to see you, Marta," she said, then laughed self-consciously, "even though I can't actually see you. But . . . you know what I mean."

Marta snuggled close to her. "I'm so glad you came. I was feeling pretty lonely. I hate being sick. It's so scary, and an awful feeling. But after I knew you were coming, I felt better."

"You *knew* I was coming?" Christina questioned. She hadn't told anyone she planned to visit Marta, only calling Katie at the last minute to ask if she could get a ride to the hospital with her.

"Yes," said Marta. "I dreamed you were coming toward me, but you couldn't reach me."

Christina's breath caught in her throat. Marta had dreamed the same dream! "Were we in a hallway?" she dared to ask.

"Yes. We were both in the hallway," Marta said. "You tried to come to me, you wanted to, but you couldn't. I thought I'd never see you again, and it made me wake up crying."

"Then how did you know I would come today?" Christina asked gently.

"Dr. Sebruch came into my room in the night," Marta said. "She heard me crying and told me not to worry. She said you were on your way."

18

The next time Christina and Katie visited the hospital, Dr. Sebruch was by Marta's bedside. Christina could somehow sense this as soon as she entered the room. Katie crossed the room to visit Rachel, who had taken Beth's old bed. Christina reached out and touched the corner of Marta's bed.

"Shhh, she's sleeping now. Our Marta is feeling poorly today," Dr. Sebruch told Christina in her low, soft accent. "It's good that you are here, Christina. Marta's operation will take place this afternoon," she went on. "It will be over in the main hospital. Can you be there when she awakens?"

"Yes. All right," Christina replied.

"Good. Bring Raindrop, if you can. It will be against hospital rules, but the kitten will do her a lot of good. So will your being there."

"I'll try to sneak him in," Christina agreed. "Doctor Sebruch, last week Marta told me you said I was coming. How did you know?"

The doctor gently took hold of Christina's arm and squeezed. "I'm a good judge of character," she said. "Stay and wait. Marta will be up soon. It will be nice for her to see you when she opens her eyes."

Christina heard Dr. Sebruch move across the room. She greeted Rachel cheerfully. Katie came to Christina's side. "Poor little Marta," she said, putting her hand on Christina's shoulder. "She looks so pale and thin."

"Paler and thinner than when we first met her?" Christina asked.

"Yeah . . . Hey, wow! She's got that rock you gave her on her bedside. Cute."

Christina heard a scratching sound coming from the direction of the closet. "I think Raindrop is trying to get out," she guessed.

"Better keep him in there," Katie said. "Nurse Worly is due to come through soon."

"You're right," Christina agreed. "I hope she doesn't hear him scratching."

"I'll start humming or something if it gets too loud," Katie said.

"Good idea. I will, too."

As if on cue, Nurse Worly bustled into the room. "Marta's still asleep, I see," she noted briskly. "Very good. She'll need all her strength for her operation. Now, Rachel, it's time for your medicine."

The kitten began scratching with determination. Katie squeezed Christina's arm anxiously and began loudly humming "Row, Row, Row Your Boat." Christina joined in.

"A little less noise, please," said Nurse Worly.

Christina and Katie stopped humming.

Scritch-scritch-scritch. Raindrop's scratching was amplified in Christina's ears by her fear that Nurse Worly would notice it. She *had* to notice it soon. It was so loud. Not knowing what else to do, Christina started humming once again. Katie joined her.

"Girls, please!" Nurse Worly said sternly.

Just then, Raindrop scampered out of the closet, under Marta's bed, and out into the middle of the room. "How did that cat get in here?" Nurse Worly cried.

Christina froze. "Has she got him?" she whispered to Katie.

"Yes," Katie replied dismally, "in her arms."

"Oh, no!" Christina moaned. "Nurse Worly," she spoke up, stepping forward. "Please let me take the cat out for you."

"No, thank you," the woman replied curtly. "I'll dispose of this fellow myself. I thought we got all the kittens out of the attic. Lord knows how long this one has been sneaking around the halls, spreading germs, animal dander, and maybe even fleas."

"What will you do with him?" Christina asked, panic filling her voice. Marta couldn't awaken to find Raindrop gone, especially not right before her operation.

"I'm putting him right out the front door. He'll be fine. He was born wild and he's survived this long." With that she headed out the door.

"I'll follow her," Katie said, talking fast. "I'll try to see where she puts him."

"Good. Go!" Christina urged her.

"I'm gone."

Christina stood by Marta's bedside wringing her hands. "Hi, Christina." A boy's voice came alongside her. "It's me, Matt. What's wrong?"

She explained about the cat and what had just happened. "I'll go down and see if I can help Katie," he offered.

"Thanks," Christina said. "It's important." Matt hurried off, and Christina was left with nothing to do but wait. Marta stirred in her sleep. She hoped the girl wouldn't awaken until Raindrop was back.

After almost fifteen minutes of waiting, Christina grew restless. What was taking them so long to return with Raindrop? Had they been able to get hold of him? What had Nurse Worly done with him? Why didn't they come back?

When she couldn't stand it any longer, she got up from the bed and groped her way to the door. Raindrop knew her. He liked her. Perhaps he'd come if she called to him. If Nurse Worly put him out, he'd probably just scramble under a bush or go some other place hidden but close by.

Keeping close to the wall, she made her way down the stairs and out the front door to the porch. "Katie? Matt?" she called softly.

No one answered. She found her way to the edge of the porch and carefully stepped down the stairs. "Raindrop," she called, feeling for the azalea bushes by the porch. "Raindrop." She let out a low whistle. "Psss, psss, psss, here, kitty. Here, Raindrop."

With her fingertips brushing the edges of the bushes and serving as a guide, she made her way around the house to the back, calling Raindrop all the while. A rustling in a nearby bush made her stop. "Raindrop? Is that you?" The leaves moved again. Some creature was definitely moving inside the bush. "Come to me, Raindrop," she coaxed. "Come on."

She followed the animal's movement for several yards along the path of the thick bushes. Then she heard it dart from the bush. Christina lunged for it. Something soft and furry brushed past her hand and then darted away. She heard a scurrying sound in the trees behind her and turned toward it.

With outstretched arms, she made her way toward the spot where she'd last heard the sound. "Aw, come on, Raindrop. Don't play games. It's me, Christina. Marta needs you. Don't run away now."

She stepped forward and, as she went to set her foot down, discovered that there was no ground underneath to meet it. She cried out as she fell forward, completely off balance.

Her shoulder hit the rocky ground first. Then she slid downhill for several yards. A tree in her path broke her slide.

Groggily, Christina lifted her head. And a hand touched her forehead.

19

"Who's there?" Christina asked in a trembling voice. "Who is it?" No one replied, although the hand remained fixed on her brow. She swiped at it, wanting to knock it away. She hit her own forehead but still felt the sensation of the hand. What was going on?

"Don't be afraid," said a woman's soothing voice.

"Who are you? What do you want?" As lovely as the voice was, Christina was still scared. She'd fallen and some stranger was down this hill with her. Getting up on her knees, she beat the air before her with trembling hands but felt nothing.

"Close your eyes, and you will see me." The woman's voice seemed to surround her. It was impossible to say from exactly what direction it came.

"What? What do you mean? I don't understand," Christina cried.

"Trust me, Christina. Close your eyes tightly and focus on the center of your darkness. You will see me. Don't be afraid. I won't harm you."

"I still don't understand." The hand was lifted from her forehead and a gentle wind ruffled Christina's hair. Somehow, she was no longer frightened. She might as well try doing what the woman wanted. It wasn't like she could spring up and run away from her.

Besides, she didn't feel the need to. Inexplicably, she felt safe with this person. The strange everywhere quality of the voice made her suspect she wasn't a regular human person. A peculiar, intense quiet had fallen over everything, making her feel like she was in some unearthly, special place.

Closing her eyes tightly, she tried to concentrate. A spot in the center of her forehead began to throb, pulsing lightly. Christina focused on it, directing all her energy to the spot.

The very smallest, yet most brilliantly bright, point of light began to pulse before her.

Light! Christina didn't want to lose it. She clamped her lids shut and crunched her face forward in her effort to hold on to the light.

The light began to expand and take form, as if it were a star coming toward her from across a vast galaxy.

"Hah!" Christina gasped, letting out a long whoosh of air as she saw what this light, this forward-rushing star, was becoming.

An angel.

An angel with wild hair as brilliant as fire; huge, arched wings aglow in a shimmer of rainbow color; flowing robes like the glistening waves of an emerald sea.

Christina was hardly aware of the joyful tears making a ribbon of wetness down her cheeks. This vision filled her with an unexplainable, irrational happiness so great it was almost more than she could hold.

The angels had not forgotten her, after all. An angel was right here, within her.

"Where have you been?" She heard the words in her own voice, even though they weren't coming from her mouth.

"With you." The voice was the same as the voice of the person whose hand had been on her forehead.

"Will I always be blind?" Christina heard herself ask. It was as if by thinking the questions, she could make the words be heard.

"You will never be blind again."

"What does that mean?" Christina asked, her thought-words sounding urgent.

"You are learning to see with different eyes, from eyes deep within yourself," the angel replied in an even, melodic voice.

"But I want to see light, to see things. Will I?"

"The light is inside you, deep inside. You can bring it forward."

"But will I see?" This time the eager words tumbled breathlessly from Christina's lips, and as they spilled into the air, the angel's image shattered, then disappeared completely.

"Wait!" Christina cried, but she was once again engulfed by complete darkness. She fell back on her heels, tired by the strain of focusing so completely on the angel.

After several minutes, her strength returned. She sensed that the angel was gone. The breeze had subsided, and the strange stillness that had surrounded her was now broken by the normal woodland sounds of birds, squirrels in the trees, and twigs snapping as small animals scurried past.

Standing, she reached out and touched a slim tree. There was nothing to do now but struggle back up the hill she'd slid down. Painstakingly, she stumbled forward, making her way from tree to tree. In a few minutes, a soft mewing sound called to her. "Raindrop," she called. "Raindrop, is that you?"

The mewing intensified. Then Christina felt a small ball of warm fur brush against her ankle. She reached down and scooped up the kitten. Why had he come to her now, when he'd run away before? she wondered. Perhaps it hadn't even been Raindrop she'd been chasing. She'd never know.

The important thing was that she had him now. She had to hurry back to Marta and show her that her kitten was safe before she went into her operation. It would mean so much to her.

When the trees ended, Christina reached out with one hand and walked with Raindrop in her other hand. She hoped she was heading toward the Children's House, but she wasn't sure.

"There you are!" Katie cried.

Christina's shoulders sagged with relief. Thank goodness.

"You found him!" Katie cried happily. "Matt, she's got him!"

Running footsteps joined them. "Christina, are you all right?" Matt asked. "Your face and hands are all muddy. What happened?"

"I slipped down the hill over there. But I'm fine," Christina replied. Oddly enough, she noticed that she felt better than fine. A new energy ran through her. She felt strong and relaxed, as if she could run a marathon race—if only she could see where she was going. Had her angel encounter given her this new strength?

"When I slid down the hill—" she began to tell of her meeting with the angel. But Katie spoke at the same time, their voices overlapping.

"I promised Marta we'd find the kitten. I'm so glad you did," she said.

Christina realized she'd have to tell Katie the story later. "We have to go upstairs and show Marta that Raindrop is safe," she said.

"Too late," Katie told her. "They've already taken her over to the main hospital, and they're getting her ready for her operation. Her mother came up to be with Marta when they took her over, and she looked so tired and worried."

"Yeah, I felt sorry for her," Matt agreed. "I'm going to go back inside. The kid I'm visiting is probably waking up now."

"Bye," Katie said. "Thanks."

"Thanks," Christina echoed. Then she turned to Katie. "I want to go over to the hospital. Dr. Sebruch said it would be good if I were there when Marta woke up, and that Raindrop should be there, too. I don't know how we can sneak Raindrop in, though."

"I know," Katie said. "We'll buy a canvas tote bag in the hospital gift shop. I know they have them because Aunt Rainie brought one home the other day after she visited a sick friend. We can stick Raindrop inside it, then fold the top over. No one will know he's in there."

"Good idea," Christina said. "On the way over, I have to tell you what just happened to me. It was the most amazing thing."

20

Christina shifted her weight on the uncomfortably stiff leather couch in the hospital waiting room while Raindrop wriggled in the tote bag on her lap. "We've been waiting forever," complained Katie, who sat next to her. "How long is this operation supposed to take?"

"I don't know," Christina admitted. "Why don't you go?"

"How would you get home?"

"Would you call my mother and ask if she'd come pick me up in a few hours?"

"All right, but will you be okay here by yourself?"

Christina nodded. "I'm in a hospital, how much safer can I be?" she joked.

"All right," Katie agreed tentatively. "Are you sure?"

"Sure. You fed Raindrop some of the tuna sandwich you bought in the hospital cafeteria, so he should be fine for a while." She noticed that the wriggling had stopped. "Is he asleep?"

"Yes. He's so cute, all curled up in the bag."

"Then everything's cool. You go."

"All right. I'll call your mother and tell her where you're waiting. If I don't come back, it means I spoke to her and she agreed to come."

"Okay. Thanks. Bye."

"Bye," Katie said.

Christina sat for a long time, waiting. She wasn't sure how long. In that time, Raindrop stirred and began crawling around. She slipped her hand into the bag and petted him, which made him purr. Though his purring sounded like a motor to her, no one said anything about it. After a while, he went back to sleep in the bag.

"Hello," a woman said, coming alongside her. The voice was somewhat familiar, but Christina couldn't place it.

"I'm sorry, but I can't see you," Christina said. "I don't know who you are."

The woman sat beside her. "Oh, that's right, I forgot. Forgive me, please. It's me, Addie Baker. The other day, in the hall, I didn't realize you couldn't see. I only found out later from some nurses who were talking."

"Oh, Ms. Baker. I'm sorry. Hello." She was glad Raindrop was asleep and hoped he stayed that way.

"I suppose you're here for Marta," Ms. Baker said.

"Yes. I want to see how her operation comes out."

"I hope she's all right. Marta is a wonderful girl. Such spirit."

"I know. She's amazing," Christina agreed.

"Speaking of spirit, I have to say I'm very impressed with your spirit as well. It takes guts to come back and continue helping the kids after a setback like yours."

"Thank you," Christina said. "It's helped me, though. It's better not to think about my own problems too much. And, you know, it's proved to me that I can get around and have a life even if I'm never . . . better."

For the first time since the accident, Christina had said aloud the thing she most feared. That she might *never* regain her eyesight. Before, she'd been afraid that saying it would make it real. But now, there it was. She'd said the words. And it *had* made the possibility seem very real. Yet somehow—perhaps because of the angel—she'd grown strong enough to deal with it.

"Have you contacted anyone about special training?" Ms. Baker asked. "Children's House has a class on reading Braille. We even have a Braille computer."

"That's reading for blind people, with raised letters?"

"Right. We can also put you in touch with groups like The Helen Keller Foundation and The Lighthouse, which have wonderful programs for people with eye problems. Have you thought about getting a Seeing Eye dog?"

"My mother mentioned it. The idea scared me at the time, but now maybe I'm more ready to do it."

Ms. Baker put her hand lightly over Christina's. "I'm sure it's all a huge adjustment for you. You don't have to go through it alone, though. These programs can really give you a lot of support and guidance."

"Oh, I'm not alone," Christina said, and saying this aloud made it also very real. "My mother's been great, and my friends have, too."

"That's wonderful," Ms. Baker said. "And I'm sure you have an angel at your shoulder, too."

Christina lifted her chin, stunned by the woman's

words. "Why do you say that?" she asked.

"Oh, just a feeling," Ms. Baker said. "Considering the fall you took, your recovery has been very fast. It could have been much worse. And you're here, worrying about a little girl. To me that shows you have a strong spirit. I can see it just looking at you. You have a certain glow about you."

"Thank you," Christina said.

"I could tell there was something special about you the moment I saw you," Ms. Baker went on. "I work with lots of people, and it's made me a good judge of character."

"Funny," said Christina. "That's what Dr. Sebruch said to me once, that she was a good judge of character."

"Doctor who?"

"Sebruch."

"I don't know him."

"Her. You must know her. She's always at Children's House. She's an Indian woman, short with long hair."

"No. We don't have any Dr. Sebruch on staff," Ms. Baker insisted in a thoughtful voice. "I'm certain of it."

"How strange," Christina said.

"It is," Ms. Baker agreed, standing. "Well, I need to go check on paperwork for a few young patients. I'll see what I can find out about Marta, then I'll be back."

"All right. Thanks," said Christina.

"You're welcome . . . oh, and . . ." She leaned in close to Christina and whispered. "As the saying goes, don't let the cat out of the bag."

Christina spread her hands across the top of the canvas tote. "I won't," she whispered back with a smile.

In a half hour, Ms. Baker returned and reported that Marta would be coming out of surgery soon. "In fact, they'll wheel her right through those double doors to your right." She called over a nurse and asked if someone could let Christina know when Marta was coming by. The nurse agreed. "Good-bye, Christina, and good luck," Ms. Baker said as she walked away.

Marta didn't come out in a half hour. At least it felt much longer to Christina. Finally, though, a nurse came by and told her that the operation was done and that Marta would be coming by soon. "In fact, here they come now," she said.

Christina heard the double doors opening on her right and instinctively snapped her head to the right, forgetting she couldn't see Marta coming.

"Huh!" she gasped hard, jumping to her feet and then staggering back against the couch.

A glowing shaft of brilliant light appeared in front of her, splitting open her darkness.

21

Christina gripped the back of the couch for support. The long line of blinding light widened in front of her. It was so bright it pained her eyes, and she jammed her palms hard into her eye sockets.

When she removed them a second later, the light had lost its blinding quality. Now it glowed in a deep brown-gold amber.

Christina saw figures coming toward her, a man and a woman both dressed in green surgical suits. They wheeled a bed between them, on which lay a small, still figure. Marta.

Beside Marta's moving bed was the same glorious angel Christina had seen in her mind's eye. She held Marta's small hand and gazed down at the little girl, never taking her eyes off her.

What was happening? Had Christina's sight returned, or was she in the grip of a vision?

The angel came closer, following the bed toward Christina. No one else seemed to be aware of the angel.

The green-garbed doctors rolled the bed, sometimes speaking to one another in serious, no-nonsense tones. As the angel approached, Christina peered at her lovely face. She knew it. She'd seen it before. Where?

The angel looked up from Marta and smiled softly at Christina.

Christina stared into her eyes—almost black, fathomless eyes with a speck of golden light—and she knew where she'd seen them before.

Dr. Sebruch!

Dr. Sebruch was an angel, and she'd been with Marta, never left her side, through the entire operation.

The doctors paused to talk to two nurses who'd hurried to the bed. As they talked, unaware of the celestial presence beside them, the angel lifted both her hands, palms up, into the air. Rays of intense white light shot out of them, reaching to the ceiling.

Christina's mouth fell open in awe as she watched, mesmerized. The angel waved her hands over Marta, spreading the beams of white light until the light wrapped Marta in a glowing, silver-white cocoon.

With her heart suddenly banging in her chest, Christina wondered what this meant. Was the angel taking Marta? Would she die?

The light hovered around Marta as Christina heard a voice in her head. "White light is healing light." The angel glanced at her again, her gentle smile warm and reassuring.

No! Marta wasn't going to die. She would get better.

The man and woman in green left, and the nurses continued wheeling Marta down the hall, not seeing the white light around her or the glorious angel at her side.

Alice came to get Christina long before they were able to visit Marta. "When did this happen?" she asked, her voice rich with happy disbelief. She cupped Christina's face and peered lovingly into her daughter's blue eyes. "When?"

"Just as they brought Marta out of the operating room," Christina said.

"Dr. Hernandez said this might happen." Alice spoke with her hands still on Christina's cheeks. "He said there might be a small amount of clot left, which would dissolve on its own. He said we should keep hoping because—"

"Mom, I saw an angel," Christina interrupted. "The angel was with Marta and she was the first thing I saw."

"An angel," Alice repeated. Normally, she didn't want to hear about angels. She didn't believe in them. But now her voice was soft, as though she were open to the possibility. "You saw an angel?"

"Yes. She was with Marta. Before that, I saw her in my mind's eye. She spoke to me and told me that if I shut my eyes tight and looked deep inside myself I'd see her, and I did. I thought she was a doctor. Remember I told you she came to visit me at the house. That was her. Mom, an angel visited me at the house."

An angel had come to her house. An angel had kissed her head and told her exactly what to do. How could she have thought the angels had forgotten her?

Alice went to a desk. "Could you page Dr. Sebruch for

me, please?" she requested. "I need to see her. It's important."

Christina joined her mother at the desk and watched as the nurse brought names up on a computer screen in front of her. "I didn't think so," the nurse said. "We have no Dr. Sebruch affiliated with this hospital. I'm sorry. Can I find someone else to help you?"

"No," Alice said. "Thank you."

"I told you," Christina said.

Alice turned to Christina, taking in her face with a long, searching gaze, then she hugged her close and hard. "My girl, my girl," she said as she started to cry.

Christina cried, too—from relief, from joy, from exhaustion.

She could see. She wouldn't spend the rest of her life in darkness. Her vision was back. She'd never take it for granted again.

"Oh, my gosh!" Alice cried out suddenly, pointing. "That bag is moving by itself."

Christina whirled around and saw the tote bag crawling across the floor toward her. "Raindrop!" she laughed, pouncing down and scooping up the bag. The kitten's small black head popped up comically.

Alice and Christina laughed. "Hi, little guy," Christina said, scratching him between his pointed ears. "It's good to see you."

After hours of waiting, Alice and Christina were able to see Marta for a very short time. Lying there in the big bed, she looked especially small and pale. Her arm was hooked to an intravenous bag on a stand. Wires taped to her chest connected her to a monitor on the side. Christina remembered the white light, now invisible to her, and told herself that her little friend would be all right.

"How do you feel?" she asked Marta.

Marta pushed her mouth into a faint smile. "Sleepy."

Christina came close and cracked open the bag with Raindrop inside. "I brought you a visitor."

Marta's smile broadened, and her dull eyes filled with light. "Raindrop! You came!" She gazed up at Christina. "Thank you for finding him."

"He found me, really," Christina said.

"Christina," Marta gasped. "You looked right at me. Can you see now?"

"Yes."

Marta breathed in happily and her eyes grew wide. "The angel did it!"

Alice stepped closer and put her hand on Christina's shoulder. "The angel?" she questioned.

Marta nodded. "While I had my operation, when I was asleep, I dreamed I saw an angel."

"Are you sure it was a dream?" Christina asked.

"I think so," Marta replied. "But she did seem very real. She talked to me and told me not to worry. I asked her to make your eyes better."

"You did?" Christina gasped.

"I hoped she would. She nodded when I asked her." Marta's voice started to trail off faintly. Christina could see she was still weak and growing tired.

"You'd better sleep," Christina said.

"Okay," Marta agreed, her voice fainter still. "Thank

you for bringing Raindrop."

"I'll keep him until you're ready to bring him home," Christina promised.

"Thanks," Marta said, her eyelids heavy, her voice a whisper. "Hey, do you know who the angel looked like, Christina?"

"Dr. Sebruch," Christina said.

"Yeah. Do you think she's an angel?"

"Yes."

"I thought so, too," Marta said just as she drifted off to sleep.

Katie sat on Ashley's front-porch steps several days later and moved her pencil intently across the lined yellow pad on her lap. Then she snapped the pencil on the pad and looked up with a self-satisfied smile as she held the pad out to Christina, Molly, and Ashley. "I was right. Look for yourselves."

Christina took the pad and gazed at the letters Katie had written. On the top line was the name *Sebruch*. Below it she'd written *cherubs*. "It's another anagram," Katie explained. "The same letters in *cherubs* are in *Sebruch*."

"I don't get it," said Molly, who sat on the step below Katie. "What are cherubs?"

"Angels!" Katie cried impatiently.

Ashley lifted her head toward the trail of horses walking out of the Pine Manor woods toward the stable. "The trail ride is coming back," she noted as she leaped down lightly from the porch railing. "There's not another one scheduled for two hours. We can take some horses out."

"Cool," said Katie, laying her pad down on the porch. "I think I'll take Daisy today."

"I'm dying to ride," Molly agreed. "Aren't you, Christina? It must be great for you to be able to ride again."

"It is, but I can't go riding with you today," Christina replied.

"We could ride out to the bridge," Ashley coaxed.

"No. Another time. Marta's leaving the hospital today. I have to bring Raindrop to her and say good-bye."

"All right," Ashley agreed.

"Say bye to Marta for me," Katie said as the girls headed toward the stable. "And tell Rachel that I'll be by to see her tomorrow. Okay?"

"Okay."

Christina went to her cabin, scooped Raindrop into the tote bag, and walked down the dirt drive to the road, where she caught the bus to the Pine Ridge Hospital. She arrived at Children's House and ran up to the second floor. She passed the open door to Ms. Baker's office. The woman looked up from the work she was doing and waved to Christina.

Since Marta's operation, Christina had come to visit Marta several times. She and Ms. Baker had talked at those times and had developed a friendship. "Marta leaves today," Ms. Baker called to Christina.

"I know," Christina replied. With a smile, she nodded toward the tote bag. "I have a little going-away gift for her."

Ms. Baker laughed and went back to her work.

In Marta's room, a slim woman with short dark hair was helping Marta pack her clothing into a suitcase open on the bed. Christina entered and waved at Rachel across the room. When she turned to Marta, she smiled, overjoyed at the change in her. The color was back in her face, and her dark eyes shined.

"Mommy, this is her," Marta said as soon as Christina stepped into the room. "This is Christina!"

"Thank you so much," Marta's mother said in a voice inflected with Spanish. "You have done so much for Marta. I don't know how to thank you."

"I loved meeting Marta. She helped me a lot, too," Christina said sincerely. With a smile, she handed Raindrop to the girl. "Here you go."

Marta hugged the kitten.

"The operation has gone very well," Marta's mother told Christina. "Better than we could have imagined. Marta's leukemia is completely gone. We will have to watch it, of course, make sure it doesn't return. But, right now, she can go back to living a normal life."

Tears of happiness sprang to Christina's eyes. At the same time, she remembered the white light the angel spread around Marta and wondered if that was the real source of the cure. "That's so great," she said, wiping her eyes and smiling.

She helped Marta and her mother continue packing. "I'll say good-bye here," Christina said when they were done. She knelt so that she was on eye level with Marta. "You be a good girl, and if you need anything, you ask for it. Ask your angel."

Marta nodded and wrapped Christina in a warm

hug. Christina gently hugged her back. "Come on, Marta," her mother said after several minutes. "We have to go."

Reluctantly, Marta let go. "I love you," she whispered. "I'll see you soon."

"I love you, too," Christina whispered back.

With a final wave, Marta followed her mother out of the room. Christina went to the window and waited a short while until Marta and her mother walked down the front-porch steps. As she watched them head down the path away from the hospital, she breathed in sharply and put her hand over her heart.

The angel, the one she'd seen the day of Marta's operation, was walking behind Marta and her mother. The angel's wings were open wide, wrapping the young girl and her mother in angelic light.

"Christina?" Ms. Baker's voice startled Christina. She turned and looked at the woman. "Sorry if I scared you," Ms. Baker said. "But a little girl has just been admitted. She's got juvenile diabetes, and it's affecting her eyesight. She's very depressed about it, and I was wondering if you could talk to her, maybe tell her about your experience losing your eyesight."

"Sure. I'll try," Christina agreed.

Ms. Baker put her hand on Christina's back. "Come on, she's in the room next to my office."

"I hope I can help her," Christina said, already trying to formulate what she'd say.

"Just being there and talking to her will be a huge help," Ms. Baker said as they walked toward the door. "I really appreciate it. You're an angel."

"No, I'm not," Christina replied. "But at least I know where to find them," she whispered silently.

FOREVER ANGELS

by Suzanne Weyn

Everyone needs a special angel . . .

Katie's Angel
0-8167-3614-6

Ashley's Lost Angel
0-8167-3613-8

Christina's Dancing Angel
0-8167-3688-X

The Baby Angel
0-8167-3824-6

An Angel for Molly
0-8167-3915-3

The Blossom Angel
0-8167-3916-1

The Forgotten Angel
0-8167-3971-4

The Golden Angel
0-8167-4118-2

The Snow Angel
0-8167-4119-0

Available wherever you buy books.

Troll